FROM ISOLATION TO COMMUNITY

YOUTH WORK IN THE COVID ERA AND BEYOND

JENNI OSBORN

ISSACHAR PRESS

INTRODUCTION

The year 2020 will go down in the history books as momentous, not only for the UK but around the whole world. Each of us knows someone who has been personally, deeply affected by the coronavirus in some way or another. As I've talked to those in the world of youth work[1] I've discovered that there has been a wide variety of responses from individuals, their organisations and their young people. Many were furloughed, some have returned to work and others are, as I write this, still on furlough. It has been an intense period of massive upheaval and change against a backdrop of fear and anxiety around the spread of the Covid-19 virus, and we are still experiencing the effects of this today.

In this book we will use a series of case studies to discuss what the impact of the coronavirus has been on our youth ministry and young people, how has Covid-19 impacted what we do, how we do it, including hearing from youth workers doing the work during the pandemic. We will also discuss what young people will need for the coming months, the crucial elements to this being stability, hope, restoration of connection to the natural world, and reconnection with their communities. The Outward

Bound Trust have, together with other organisations which prioritise the way people interact with the natural world, written a report in the importance of outdoor education calling for a holistic approach to building resilience and hope in our young people.

The aftershock of that first lockdown period as well as many other political and social shocks we have witnessed in this year will continue to be felt. Those shocks have included: the rise of Black Lives Matter protests after the death of George Floyd, and many other black people, at the hands of the police in the US; the increasing awareness of the climate crisis, revealed by the cessation of manufacturing and driving and flights globally due to the pandemic; the poor handling of the UK exam results by the Department for Education; and the subsequent demand that students attend university in person, only for them to be put in self-isolation within the first week of term.

In addition to all that, here in the UK we are on the brink of leaving the EU partnership with little detail available that reassures the public about the impact of adding in more border checks for our people, our medicines, or our food.

Whatever happens in the next 12 months, it's safe to say that Brexit and Covid-19 are the defining issues of this generation, creating a tidal wave which will impact the lives of adults and young people alike for many years to come.

One organisation I spoke to, KICK, based in London have seen their work in schools, providing PE lessons, mentoring and chaplaincy to children and young people, not dry up during the first period of lockdown as might be expected, but increase as schools became providers of childcare for key worker children.

Another organisation, The Outward Bound Trust, told me about the pride they have in their staff who, having been put on furlough, have got involved in their local communities -including one who is now managing their local foodbank voluntarily.

I am aiming to show just how broad the response has been in the youth work world and how different organisations have all played a role in continuing to support young people and children across the country. I aim tom do this by giving you examples of good practice. We will also see those who have felt especially vulnerable and have struggled to know just how to respond. Many of those I spoke to expressed feeling a huge responsibility for their staff teams as well as the young people they work with and this often felt destabilising.

There were other similarities from one setting to another. Nearly every youth work organisation has tried video conferencing with their groups of young people. Nearly everyone has also quickly realised that, despite our teenagers generally being labelled digital natives, video conferencing via Zoom (so abundant that the word 'zoom' has come to mean generic video calling, even if it's actually using a different platform[2]) has been largely rejected by them.

Several of the people I spoke had had more success with this that others. The Red Balloon Foundation were one of these who have only found 'Zoom fatigue' setting in with the November lockdown, whereas KPC Youth had a more immediate negative response to their digital engagement.

There are also significant differences where organisations have responded to the local picture with activity boxes, seed boxes, online gaming sessions, online cooking sessions, detached or street-based work and a projection project,(using a projector to amplify young people's voices onto local landmarks), to name but a few.

There are also many reports of the delight of young people when their youth workers have made the effort to keep in touch through postcards, doorstep visits, and deliveries of wellbeing packages. While it was possible in the summer of 2020, face-to-face, socially distanced group gatherings also took place. Another similarity has been the theme of collaboration with other youth work providers in the area - both the detached projects I spoke to have experienced this with Steve from Sidewalk in Scarborough telling me

"This hasn't always felt comfortable but it has been worth doing and I think this is something we'll prioritise in the future."

One other similarity was the provision of food. The majority of the community-based projects I spoke to had connections with local food providers, such as foodbanks or other similar donation led schemes. In some situations, the involvement with this provision was young people led. These young people and youth workers have been experiencing what it is to go from isolation to community in a very tense and uncertain time.

For those youth worker managers who have responsibility for teams as well as young people, it has been a deeply unsettling and uncertain time. In truth everyone has had to deal with the same set of circumstances and very few have managed to stay entirely positive through all the challenges of lockdowns. These were often last minute changes that have had to be implemented within hours of announcement against the backdrop of the UK government disagreeing with their own independent group of scientists on the appropriate course of action.

In September 2020, members of the Scientific Advisory Group for Emergencies (SAGE) proposed a "short sharp 'circuit breaker' lockdown... Instead, ministers imposed a 10pm curfew"[3] In fact England didn't go into a another lockdown until November. When 3 tiers of restrictions were first announced on 12th Oct the Chief Medical Advisor immediately stated that tier 3 restrictions would not be enough to curb infection rates.

Tier 4 was not introduced until 20th Dec when it became clear that the government's plan to allow 3 households to mix for 5 days over Christmas would cause a dangerous spike in infection rates nationally at a time when the R rate of transmission was already climbing fast due to the new strain of the virus found in Kent.

This book has been written November 2020 – January 2021, and so covers the period of time from the first and starkest lockdown across the whole UK , (March 2020 - May 2020). This included keeping the majority of school children at home, with different restrictions being gradually lifted at different times in the four nations of the UK.

We then had a second period of significant restrictions, colloquially called Lockdown 2, in November 2020. This did not include keeping children at home. At the time of writing in January 2021 we were in a more substantial Lockdown 3 with the majority of children learning from home.

The reality is that it is all about managing risk, at both the national and local level. Those working with children and young people know about risk management, it having formed a key part of the work for a long time now, and rightly so. This is a whole new level and many of those I spoke to expressed frustration at how the national or local guidelines for managing the Covid-19 risk seemed to overlook the risk to mental health and wellbeing of young people and youth workers that comes with self-isolation and lack of physical contact with others. One young person who had been experiencing mental illness prior to the pandemic said

> *"Self-isolating and social distancing was a bad habit I worked really hard to get out of. Now being made to do it and being told it's the right thing to do. It's very confusing and I'm sacred of falling back into that cycle"*[4]

Everyone is uncertain about what the future will hold, from those in decision-making positions to those who are the recipients of the services offered. The National Youth Agency (NYA)[5] have done an excellent job at lobbying for youth workers to gain essential workers status, getting clear information and guidance out to youth work organisations, and responding quickly when the government have made last-minute changes.

They have increasingly become the pillar of youth work practice in England, with some of the organisations I spoke to saying that they had not referred to the NYA previously, but have found their guidance to be invaluable during these most testing of times.

The future may be uncertain but work is going on right now to ensure that our young people and children have a future to look forward to, that they can lift their heads above the here and now to catch a glimpse of something brighter. In the final chapter of this book, we will look at some of that work, and give you an idea of how to offer that hope, both within a faith context and in a secular context. Hope is the oil that keeps the engine of our souls running, for us, for our young people and children, for everyone, everywhere.

CHAPTER 1

STRENGTHEN COMMUNITY - WORKING IN SCHOOLS

In March 2020 the tightest restrictions to the movement of people in over a generation was imposed and, most unusually of all, schools were told they must close to all pupils except 'key worker' children. The definition of 'key workers' changed a little during the lockdown but largely included those whose parents work in the NHS and other 'frontline' services, in supermarkets and delivery services such as Royal Mail and others.

There was no expectation that the children in school would receive education, though schools were expected to ensure the children at home were receiving work to complete and send back. Schools quickly put rotas in place to ensure there were enough staff in school to cover the children who were in attendance, providing them with a safe space to be while their parents worked hard. It has been an incredibly turbulent time for anyone involved in school communities, with the rate of change picking up speed in an incredible way.

The vast majority of youth and children's work that had been provided by outside agencies during school time and on school premises up until that point stopped. I have spoken to many schools workers all over the country and so many of them have seen their work stop and not get started again even when schools opened again in September 2020. However, there are still organisations delivering work in schools and we'll hear from three of them here, one providing much needed PE and outdoor education to schools in London, one whose work wasn't in schools before the pandemic but has now become mainly school-based and another supporting autistic children and young people[1] in schools. So what has been happening in our schools during this challenging year?

Increased Support in Schools During Lockdown

Headed up by Joe Lowther, KICK have seen an exponential growth to their schools work in the 6 years since Joe joined the organisation. 6 years ago. Crucially, as the schools lockdown was announced in March 2020, and the trustees at KICK were trying to figure out what this might mean for the charity, the phone calls made to schools were met with head teachers being absolutely resolute that KICK should continue to be in their schools. In one instance the school requested more of their time, so they went from one session a week to three.

So, what is it that KICK offer? KICK is an organisation that began in London with a mission to see children and young people's lives transformed with God's love through sport and support. KICK offers 4 professional services in schools: Physical Education, Street Dance, Solution Focussed Mentoring and Chaplaincy. They have 56 staff who are from a mix of backgrounds across sport and education, all qualified coaches who run PE curriculum involving 12 different sports and 12 different dance disciplines in primary schools, and offer the mentoring and chaplaincy in primary and secondary schools.

Alongside this they train church volunteers to run KICK Academies. One church in particular were so committed to the young people in their patch that they agreed to change their Sunday service times in order to run a KICK Academy on a Sunday morning after church - that meant children and young people could be at home to have Sunday lunch with their families.

KICK have worked in 58 out of 70 schools throughout lockdown. Add to this the expansion of their summer programme of KICK Camps from 30 days to 140 days. This was after another charity encouraged KICK to enable more children and young people to get back into physical activity having been cooped up at home and not being out and about for so long. The picture for the team at KICK is therefore one that bucks the trend of so many schools work organisations in 2020.

How have they done this? KICK is a brilliant example of an organisation that has a very specific aim, who have got excellent relationships with the schools they serve, and who have taken an approach that brings real, tangible benefit to the young people and children they encounter. The amazing thing is that they have expanded their vision. There is now the opportunity for other cities and towns around the UK to join the KICK network and have a KICK presence in schools and churches local to you[2]. The feedback from schools is impressive and varied. This is just one example from a school in Twickenham.

> "The school has had the privilege of receiving support from KICK. Will, the mentor, has had a significant impact on each and every one of the children.
> All of the children were vulnerable and hard to reach...The impact has been so great it has enabled children who were struggling to re- engage and make progress. Particularly under current situations, this type of provision for the children will be vital to prevent a huge issue with mental health and school disadvantage gaps in progress increasing." (Headteacher, St Stephens School, Twickenham).

Working Outdoors

It is clear that the work that KICK do in schools is well regarded and that the presence of their staff in schools is significant. What makes KICK stand out from the rest is clearly their offer of sport provision, at a time when fewer schools than ever before have specialist PE teachers on their staff. This opportunity for schools to benefit from professional coaches across a range of different sports disciplines is a goldmine for head teachers.

However, it's not all about the sport per se, it's about what sport offers our young people: exercise, fresh air, movement, discipline, learning new skills, support of team mates and investment of an adult's time in them.

It's also about finding a way to bring something to school that's much needed, in education this is called 'added value'. What value can be added over and above that of the lessons they receive. It includes things like additional music provision, the opportunity for children and young people to take part in a show or play, the potential for using outdoor space to grow things for eating or enjoying, the provision of a library – or structured use of the library the school might already have.

Right now, these are all things that the schools are often struggling to provide, education in the covid era is a very different picture to that from pre-covid times. But they will be needed, and, one might argue, all the more so as we emerge from the depths of a covid winter.

Another organisation that has not traditionally worked in schools but has found itself doing more in partnership with local schools is the Outward Bound Trust. If you recognise the name it's probably because they are one of the biggest providers of residential trips for young people particularly in the North of England, Snowdonia and Scotland. They are experts in delivering high level adventure and learning experiences in the mountains, taking young people away from their usual urban environments.

This has had to change, as is true for all of the organisations I've spoken to. Since September 2020, Outward Bound have been into schools to deliver outdoor education that is "Safe, Simple and Fun". In the period between September and December 2020 the Trust worked with over 3,000 young people and children in a non-residential context, through their Adventure Days and in-school programmes. Their chief executive says

"These sessions are providing a life-line to many young people, offering freedom, respite and the chance to be active and socialise in a Covid-safe way."[3]

Outward Bound have also been working hard to encourage governments around the UK to understand the role that outdoor education plays in the overall mental health and wellbeing of young people and children. They have done a huge amount in this area and we'll hear more about that in other chapters.

Communication is Key

For other schools work organisations 2020 has been a very challenging year. Frequently this means the furloughing of staff in the short term and redundancies in the longer term as schools have started back again but with a very restricted timetable, that often does not include the possibility of visitors. As every school has been allowed to interpret the guidelines themselves, there are some notable exceptions to this, where schools have been able to prioritise therapeutic work in certain settings. One organisation currently working in schools is ReachOutASC.

ReachoutASC is a team of specialist teachers who go into schools in the Lancashire and the North West to build programmes around individual autistic students. They design programmes around the principle of "Getting It Right for Me", specifically looking at how to make the school experience better for autistic students.

They work in both primary and secondary schools. In primary schools the team are working with teaching and support staff to train them in techniques for dealing with autistic students in class.

In secondary schools they are working directly with students to help them understand their autism. They produce lots of resources for use with students in one-to-one or group work. These explore topics like the social world and the context for conversation and events in the community, using lots of creative ways of communicating. Communication is a key area where autistic people can struggle, at the same time as non-autistic people may struggle to communicate with autistic children because the way the autistic brain works is different.

Where schools and other organisations rely heavily on written or verbalised communication, this can be a minefield for an autistic person to navigate. So ReachoutASC use lots of different techniques to communicate. They aim to help children understand themselves and be happy in who they are, giving them confidence and hope! Hope is an absolutely essential thing to be able to offer our young people, across the spectrum of ability, hope is what keeps us going, and enables us to look to the future albeit cautiously! As much as this is true for us as adults, it is also true for our young people.

It's hard for autistic children to imagine what something might look like in the future and so they tend more than others to catastrophise (to assume the worst will happen). What we can do is put some certainty in place - which looks like hope. Lynn and her team love to encourage children to look for hope in their current situation so that they can build a positive picture of hope for their own lives.

Lynn and her team's work is based on the work of Professor Damian Milton on the Double Empathy theory. This theory suggests that when people with very different experiences of the world interact with each other, they will struggle to empathise with each other. Non-autistic people can catch a glimpse of how this feels for autistic people whenever we try to talk to someone who does not share our first language, or even when the person we talk to does not share the same interest in the topic under discussion. Imagine how much more frustrating and isolating it is for autistic people, who have this experience every time they communicate[4].

In school kids can get into trouble when they don't fit in with the framework of communication. So teachers need to be encouraged to really hear what the children are trying to say. ReachoutASC's approach is to come alongside and ask 'what works with this child?' and build on that, so that teachers feel supported and encouraged to really think about how to connect with their children.

Strengthen Community

Schools are very close to my own heart and I love to hear about the work being done to 'support and scaffold' the education that is happening in our schools. Right now, we continue to see the Covid-19 pandemic impact on more or less every detail of the school day, from the length of lessons, to the way lunchtimes are run, to the need for Perspex screens in the staffroom and so on. As a result the role of visitors in schools has often fallen by the wayside. There is just too much else going on, and too many potential problems with inviting visitors in.

However, as we have seen in this chapter and will continue to see in other chapters of the book, there are organisations whose presence in schools has been integral to the reopening of schools and to the strengthening of the community during a time of isolation.

CHAPTER 2

WILDERNESS PROPHETS - DETACHED YOUTH WORK STORIES

What makes detached youth work stand out from the other contexts of youth work delivery is the intentional act of going to the young people. We find them 'where they are at' rather than putting on a programme in a centre and having them come to the youth work. Detached work often involves working with those who are socially excluded, those who do not want to engage with adults, those who are "too wary or too deeply estranged to accept... even the slight commitment required by club membership"[1]

The work takes place, in the main, on the street, but also in other public spaces where young people have chosen to be. Detached youth work then is more accessible to young people, especially to those who are not likely to attend youth activities in a building or centre.

Detached youth work has often been seen as the 'difficult' end of youth work, involving spending lots of time hanging around often in the dark and cold or wet weather in order to 'bump into' young people who are reluctant to engage with youth work activity or adults in general.

During the Covid-19 pandemic however, this street-based way of working has really become popular. The Federation of Detached Youth Work, in partnership with the National Youth Agency (NYA), have provided guidelines for the work[2] prioritising street-based or detached youth work since they were successful in lobbying the government to designate youth workers as essential workers during the pandemic.

This chapter will focus on the detached work done by two different organisations who have been doing this kind of youth work since the halcyon days of pre-covid. One organisation is based in the centre of Newcastle, specifically the Byker and Walker estates. I spoke to Dave who heads up MINE youth, and was equally fascinated by their values and principles as well as the work which flows out from those. MINE youth are the only youth work project I've come across so far who delivered an outdoor holiday club provision in December.

As he reflected on the year of 2020 Dave has realised that "I've been glad for the chance to step back and ask the big questions. "Who are we? What are we about? What is our role in the community in this crazy year?"[3]. These are all really critical questions to be asking, as we'll see in the final chapter of this book. The other conversation was with Steve Blower from Sidewalk in Scarborough. Whenever I talk to Steve I am really impacted by his passion and quiet thinking through of why they do their youth work using a pre-dominantly street based approach. They use the Asset Based Community Development method that is so important in community building, because it sends a clear message to the young people that they meet: you matter, you are an asset to your community.

Steve gave me quite a lot of detailed reflection on two elements of the work of Sidewalk during covid-19 – the projector project and collaborative working, but first here's a bit of background on the work they do.

Disrupting the persistent narrative

Sidewalk, Scarborough started as a detached youth work project set up by local churches in the town. They have since added other strands of work into the project but remain a detached youth project at their heart. Sidewalk view the young people they interact with as *wilderness prophets*. They have found new ways of thinking and being in community. They are always asking 'what if' and use their voices to stand up for those who are marginalised, discriminated against and ostracized.

The persistent narrative about young people has been either that they are anti-social or vulnerable and weak. These perspectives should be challenged by a more positive asset-led approach which locates young people within a bigger social context. Rather than targeting work around a specific symptom of behaviour, an asset-led approach acknowledges that it's much better to look at what's causing the problem than merely treating the symptom.

Steve's reflections on being a leader during this time are recognisable to many I would imagine, and replicated across other youth work managers experiences. He spoke about feeling a sense of panic and the huge weight of responsibility for staff and young people. He talked about the need to continue the reflections, being aware that a lot of youth work practice during this Covid-19 era has had to be about keeping busy, being able to respond and react quickly to significant changes in the law and guidance.

It is vital that we take stock, stopping to carve out time for reflection and not just allowing ourselves to get swept up in the ever-increasing speed of work. Let's not let the Covid-19 speed of response become normal. This is something we'll come back to because I believe it will be more important than ever before.

Case Study: Projecting Young People's Voices

Steve and the team had already been considering movie nights at the skate parks so the idea of doing outdoor projection was not an unusual thought. This led to considering using outdoor projection technology to display young people's words. The skate park locally is at the bottom of a high cliff, so the detached team would go out with a question to ask the young people, mainly about their reactions to Covid-19 restrictions and experiences, which would then be projected. With their responses onto the cliff side.

The team were also keen to gather any other pieces for display, creative writings or reflections (in first lockdown), second lockdown was peer-to-peer support messages of hope or advice from one group of young people to another. In between lockdowns, late summer time, the projector would be set up under a bridge or in an alleyway initially to promote conversation with passers-by. Teams of two or three youth workers would go out with the projector, one to look after the projector and the others to chat to passers-by, who would often be people who wouldn't always engage with young people. Steve told me:

> *The beauty of this project is that it gives young people an amplified voice,*
> *an affirmation of their existence, a sense of acceptance and words worthy of*
> *'projecting' in every sense of the word.*

As a result of the projection project, the approach to detached work has been adapted. Where it used to be different teams walking around the community, they are now working from wherever the projector is set up and young people are gathering around that venue. Also due to covid restrictions the teams have not been mixing so much. The same team members are meeting the same young people in the different spots where the projector is set up.

This has led to deeper and more consistent relationships being formed with young people.

Collaboration and Change

Steve also told me about other centre-based work they did in collaboration with other youth work providers in Scarborough, which he said was an interesting experience. In fact, this sharing of ideas and collaboration has been a theme in the way they have seen practices changing during covid. There is more collaboration, especially as detached youth work has become the main way of delivering youth work during covid.

This has not all been easy. Sidewalk have a very specific rationale for working on the streets, and they have a clearly defined set of values including seeing the young people they work with as bringers of change and young wilderness prophets who carry the seeds of change within them.

This is not true of all those organisations who have found themselves delivering street-based youth work during this time. Throughout this book we are hearing from organisations whose work has moved young people from isolation to community during this covid era. Sidewalk are one organisation who were already doing this by embracing the building of community by and for young people themselves.

Young People's Voices

We need the voices of young wilderness prophets, in our society at large but also in our churches. Too many times young passionate voices are dismissed simply because of their youth or passion, because they do not talk the 'same language' as the PCC or the diaconate, or the senior leadership in schools. We need adults to nurture and amplify these voices, not to mould them into a 'softer' version of themselves and not to dismiss them as irrelevant. This year has shown us more than ever before that we need our young people to stand up and use their voices to bring change, no matter how uncomfortable that may feel for us adults.

Pop-up Street Clubs

MINE Youth, Newcastle is a primarily detached youth work project, with a strong commitment to building relationships with young people that last for the long term. The street based work in Byker and Walker leads into semi-structured group work but these sessions are always based on what young people say they want to do, so frequently change in theme.

They have strong faith connections with churches in the area and with Scripture Union, a national youth and children's charity which focuses on supporting faith-based youth ministry. As the first lock-down began MINE found that moving to online groups was almost impossible to do. Only one group kept going, which was a 'Bible and Board Games' group. This group involves young people from 2 or 3 families and they soon found that board games still work over video calling platforms and so they continued. But besides this, MINE were also offering packs of craft or activities that could be shared online. Their Facebook page quickly became a space for sharing successes and suggestions for what else could be added to the packs.

Case Study: Restarting

In May 2020 MINE were able to restart the detached work. This was just Dave and one other team member at this point, covering the two estates. They were finding young people who shouldn't be out but they were usually just in pairs or threes. These were kids who couldn't stay at home, home was not a safe place for them to be.

Dave and his team were making much needed contact to ensure that young people knew they were not forgotten. As the summer wore on, most of the usual summer events were cancelled or postponed in Newcastle and further afield.

MINE continued with their detached work, able to give out food and/or activity packs and also hold pop-up street clubs that were encouraging young people to get active and spend some time, safely, outdoors. They had a great time connecting with loads of young people in the Byker area. Dave said,

> *"It's been a fantastic wonderful summer. We've got to spend the time with some brilliant young people in Byker and Walker and we're really looking forward to what comes next."*

Once the NYA guidance came out that said groups could be 15 young people plus leaders, MINE began their Sports and Faith club again, along with a new club that is led by those young people who came along to the pop-up events in the summer.

When blurred lines are a good thing

One of the strands to MINE Youth's work is training of junior leaders. They run a programme for those who want to learn more about leadership and working with young people. Often those on this trainee scheme are still teenagers themselves. which often leads to a blurring of the lines between young people and junior leaders.

MINE sees this as a positive thing. It shows that young people's voices are important, and that being part of the community is about relationship rather than achievement or doing things a certain way. The investment in these junior leaders is immense, and rightly so, as young people step into a role that is more structured. It requires a certain level of responsibility, but never without support and encouragement from the rest of the team. The young person who has become the latest recruit to the scheme this year has already successfully bid for funding for a garden project. This is one sign of this young persons emerging development into a leadership role.

Some of the values of MINE Youth are especially critical in this context. The value of fellowship, which is about building good and positive relationships for everyone who belongs to MINE. The value of growth, acknowledging that everyone has worth as they are but also that everyone can learn, whether they are an adult or a young person. And finally the value of hope, the commitment to talk hopefully about the area they live and work in. I get the sense that this is important for those children and young people connected to MINE, who perhaps don't hear this from others around them.

Reflections

Detached youth work has become really prevalent this year. It's great to hear that more organisations are prepared to adapt their practices in order to maintain the relationships they have with local young people as well as growing the numbers they have contact with.

Arguably, there's an authenticity to this approach which is entirely different to centre-based work. This is not youth work that seeks to distract young people from or curb certain behaviours, this is not about adults controlling the spaces and setting down boundaries. This is youth work that truly meets young people where they are at, where boundaries are fluid and where the young people call the shots.

The asset based approach mentioned by Steve has real strength in the view it takes of young people and the spaces they inhabit in the local community. It's not without its challenges, relationships can be fluid and inconsistent, successes might be measured in positive interactions. While the goal is always that young people's voices will be heard and acted upon by those who hold the decision-making power in the local community, that kind of success is rare.

The asset based approach is one we will continue to discuss in other chapters, there is much to be said for using this as a model for youth work, especially youth work practice that seeks to build community.

CHAPTER 3

FAITH AS ITS PURPOSE - CHURCH BASED YOUTH WORK STORIES

There has been an ongoing debate in the world of church or faith based youth work training and thinking about the 'youth work' or 'youth ministry' terminology. It's an argument that is too big to tackle here, and is perhaps a needless splitting of hairs in any case. I have been using the term 'youth work' in this book, but here in this chapter it might be more appropriate to use that interchangeably with the term 'youth ministry'. The latter has faith as its purpose and message and is very specifically the kind of youth work one might find in a Church-based context.

The world of youth ministry is one I'm very familiar with, it being where I began. It is also where many youth work practices were honed. The church in the UK begun to recognise the importance of working with young people through The Boys Brigade, the YMCA and the Children's Special Service Mission, which later become Scripture Union, as early as the late 1800's.

Within a few years the Inter-Varsity Fellowship had begun along with the Crusaders, now known as Urban Saints and of course, the Boy Scouts. Baden-Powell, the founder of the Boy Scouts, was a contemporary of Kurt Hahn whose belief in the central principle of outdoor education being critical for young people led to the foundation of Gordonstoun School, where a young Prince Charles was educated. It also led to the creation of the Outward Bound Trust.

Now let's turn our attention to youth ministry as practised in a significant number of churches across the country. Youth ministry is a peculiar animal in the world of youth work. Many groups have low numbers of teenagers, many youth workers/ministers are responsible for children and families as well as for young people. Tim Gough, Pioneer Youth For Christ Director for Wales and the editor of YouthWorkHacks.com, talks about the pressures of working as a youth worker for a church as like being in the middle of an hourglass.

Above the youth worker is not only their line manager, usually the church leader, but also the many others who feel invested in some way in the youth worker such as parents. others on the church leadership team and other members of the church. Below the youth worker are all the people they are responsible for. This includes young people but also a team of volunteers, some of whom are also parents or otherwise included in the group above them as well.

It's a unique position for a youth worker to have as their context for work, and can create pressure. Add in the intricacies of worshipping in the same church as you work in, which is the normal expectation. All of this plus living within the same community and the pressures we have from our own expectations - that hourglass can be a very uncomfortable space to occupy.

Youth ministry has been struggling with funding problems, as well as resourcing issues like clergy burnout and the volunteer crisis in some churches. There is diminishing national support from events such as *Youth Work the Conference* and *Soul Survivor,* both of which have stopped running in recent years. The conference space has been filled by the *National Youth Ministry Weekend*[1] and the hole left by the ceasing of Soul Survivor camps is also being filled, (Covid dependent,) by *Satellites*[2], due to launch in Summer 2021.

Both of these initiatives are led by Youthscape. They are passionate and highly articulate about supporting youth ministers in their work with young people. The respect that they have earned means that they are one of the best placed organisations to enable these major events in the youth ministry calendar. For those working in the Church of England, there is often good support available from the Diocese and the same is true in several other denominations across the country.

However, the struggle has been exacerbated by Covid-19 and meant that youth ministry staff may have made a lower key response to the pandemic than some other youth organisations with a wider remit. Listening to what youth ministers are saying has allowed me to identify five reasons for this lower key response:

Tradition

Case Study: New in Post

Lucy Skelton of St James' in Clitheroe was new in post in January 2020 and found herself bringing a very different flavour of youth work to the post. Lucy's style of facilitating activities and encouraging open discussions was so different that it felt to her as if the young people were in shock. They were having to do things for themselves and this was new!

However, Lucy credits one particular activity with having really broken through the initial reluctance of the young people to get on board with this new way of working: the youth band. The previous leader of the youth band said that they needed to stop leading and so Lucy took it on. She doesn't play in the band (though she is a musician) but gives all the agency to the young people.

For the first few weeks they were unsure what to do with this, they were not used to being able to choose whichever songs they thought were appropriate to record for the services when they were leading. Lucy got them rehearsing more often, mentored the drummer and welcomed any young person who said they would like to play or sing.

It's a very 'School of Rock' story, but shows all over again the power of music and tradition-breaking to bring people together and make a big difference to young people. Lucy told me

> *"For the Christmas Show they learned 10 new songs and how to set up the sound, nearly all the young people were involved. They worked so hard and I am so proud of them"*

Churches tend to towards resting on their traditional practices perhaps more than most - this is also true in youth ministry. These traditions might look like youth club in the building every Friday night, or providing Sunday School for the teenagers every Sunday. With the pandemic arriving in the UK in February 2020, the church response has often been to move this same pattern to the online space. This is a big shift for many churches who have resisted moving to online provision up until now. It is also a steep learning curve which also creates its own pressure and stress.

Resources (finance and volunteer base)

Some churches are in the enviable position of being financially secure with plenty of resources to give to their youth ministry programmes and personnel.

Many, however, have suffered the knock-on effect of austerity measures put in place in the aftermath of the 2008 crash. Budgets are squeezed and along with other factors, this has been a driving factor in the reality that many youth ministry jobs are part-time. Not only are the finances often a challenge, but there is also a challenge in the traditional volunteer base of church life.

This again has multiple factors including:

- Decreasing numbers attending church
- More adults having to work and in some cases do more than one job
- change in attitude to church life as a whole - such as, most Sundays but not every Sunday.
- the willingness of volunteers is often tied to the personality of the leader who is asking for assistance,
- burnout among clergy and other church leaders (including youth leaders!) is a real problem, as is the rate of church leaders being disgraced in some way or other.

Those church members who willingly volunteered for someone, who turns out to have been covering up abusive behaviour, are likely to be disillusioned even if they haven't been affected by the abuse. Their capacity to keep volunteering will be diminished.

People also move away, become ill, become the main childcare support for adult children, and so on and so forth.

Case Study: The Importance of Resources

Loyd Harp from Holy Trinity Church in Rudgwick, Horsham told me about one of the groups he has been running which required a complete change of volunteer leadership during the summer of 2020, when groups could begin meeting up again.

The other interesting thing about the Rudgwick Youth Centre is their space. Unusually for church-based youth work, they have dedicated use of an old cricket pavilion which stands on the playing fields in the centre of Rudgwick. Their youth work is able to use the football fields as well as the woodland behind the centre. They have not been able to go back to their church building at any point during the past year but this has not been catastrophic because they have a lot of outdoor space they can and do use.

Health

This is a potential issue for all of the youth workers I have come across in the course of writing this book. However, only one told me about his worries about his own health as he is in the vulnerable category.

Alastair Middlemist, at Maidstone Baptist Church, has been juggling the youth ministry role with a church leader role and a health condition which makes him especially vulnerable to covid-19. This has meant keeping all the groups he is involved in online, with only those run by volunteers opening in the summer of 2020.

He reflects that he is glad to have keep in regular contact with the vast majority of their young people, recognising that this is not always the case for those whose only contact is through Zoom.

Confusion about the guidelines and regulations

As has been said elsewhere, the National Youth Agency (NYA) have done a lot of work on producing guidelines for those in youth work. Not every church is aware of the NYA and the work they do in supporting those who work with young people.

It seems that different diocese and other national denominations have responded to the changing guidelines in different ways. It is completely understandable that one of the defining aspects of the covid era has been confusion over the speed of changes to guidelines and regulations.

This coupled with the four nations of the UK having their own local responses has meant that lockdowns have happened at different times, support bubbles have meant differing groups, rule of six has included children but not everywhere.

I had a conversation with a home-educating Mum, a long-standing friend of mine, in the autumn of 2020 in which we both expressed frustration at churches who were not allowing in person gatherings for our teenage children despite it being within the guidelines that were in place at the time. Of course, this all has to be held in tension with other factors - health of leaders is a key aspect of any discussion as well the size of space available. Another source of uncertainty is the NYA's use of the phrase 'vulnerable young people' in their guidelines about continuing youth work during lockdowns. They were intentional about not defining who was vulnerable, leaving this to different organisations to define themselves.

My own opinion is that all young people could be classed as vulnerable right now. If we take a number of areas into consideration such as family life, mental health, learning needs and existing support networks then the potential for vulnerability becomes clear.

This pandemic will continue to have a long-term impact on our young people, more so than for other age groups, and this puts the majority of them, if not all, into a 'vulnerable' category – an opinion I have heard reflected in both church based youth ministry and in non-faith-based youth work contexts.

Numbers of young people

Church youth groups are often low numbers of young people covering a wide age range and often includes siblings. This is of course not always true; some have larger groups than others and that can bring its own pressures as well as rewards for youth ministers.

There are also a number of reasons why churches have fewer numbers of young people, which have been covered extensively in other writings about youth ministry. In his book *Faith Generation*, Nick Shepherd talks about the declining numbers and how this has been seen as 'normal' for many decades, with the expectation that young people, needing to 'find their own identity' as adolescents will eventually return to church as adults.

That this has not happened for a significant period of time shows that:

> *"Youth ministry must play a role in helping make faith plausible in the modern world and helping young people establish their own Christian presence."*[3]

Reflective practice

Where youth leaders in churches have done training, they have often been introduced to reflective practice and encouraged to incorporate this into their working practices. Loyd and I talked about how that works in his setting, whereas another youth minister told me "We haven't done any reflections, I think we're just trying to survive!"

As we head into a third lockdown in January 2021, it becomes all the more important to reflect on what worked well in the previous year, in order to figure out what might be useful to carry on with. We are all hoping that this third lockdown will be the last one before vaccinations are rolled out and the pandemic retreats. But from where we are currently, that's almost impossible to predict.

In conversations with youth ministers in different churches around the UK I have heard some great stories about what they have been doing. From socially distanced Christmas dinners and a virtual nativity to wide games outdoors and scavenger hunts on Zoom.

From a youth band to an art therapy group, from delivering activity packs for all young people to putting together Bible Study videos for young people. There's been a lot of innovation required at the drop of a hat.

I have heard many say: "I did not know how to be a youth minister without being able to see young people face to face". It has been a challenging time for so many!

Reflections

As the UK moves through its third lockdown period within less than a year and we hear talk of tightening the rules even further, there is no question that the current situation is dire. It's all the more challenging because this is the third time.

We've had to juggle since March 2020 and make dramatic wholesale changes to our practice. Youth ministry is not alone in making such changes, it is not alone in lamenting the lack of face-to-face connections with young people, it is not alone in having had to negotiate changes that have had to be implemented quickly.

There is however something unique about youth ministry which has to do with that hourglass image we talked about earlier in the chapter. While some have found themselves in a well-balanced situation with appropriate accountability and support from across their congregation, for others their work has much harder to negotiate anyway and the pandemic has made it even harder.

CHAPTER 4

EMBEDDED - YOUTH &
COMMUNITY WORK STORIES

Community-based youth work has grown out of the statutory sector of UK youth work. Over the years successive governments have made different decisions about the importance of working with young people, resulting in differing levels of funding as well as changes to the underlying ideology of youth work.

The most recent change of focus has been the setting up of the National Citizenship Service and apprenticeships, meaning that any statutory-funded project that doesn't run one or other of these programmes lost their funding.

So now there are youth work organisations. who were often funded fully or partly by the local council or a statutory body, that have become charities with grant-based funding.

These are organisations embedded in their local community. They are relied upon by a whole swathe of that community, from the young people themselves to their parents, their social workers and other stakeholders in that locality.

I have spoken to a number of youth work organisations across the country who are passionate about supporting the young people in their care, despite the seemingly endless changes to funding that have happened in recent years and the changes brought by the pandemic.

One is based in Cardiff and has music creation and production at its core of activities in more 'normal' times, but has has been doing something very different during the pandemic. Another is up the road in Bridgend, facing a downward trend in the engagement from their local young people and still figuring out how to reverse that.

I also spoke to a London based youth service who offer support and training for young people having difficulties in school, at home or in the community, helping them to reengage with employment, education or training.

And finally I talked to a project in Dundee, working in a church building right in the heart of the city centre. They began life as a project of the church and still retain a positive relationship with them, but have now moved to independent charity status.

Growing food in Wales

In Cardiff, Grassroots is a city centre, open access youth provision which was open Monday – Friday pre-Covid-19, working with a diverse range of young people. As well as offering a drop in service for those young people experiencing various challenges such as employment and training, housing needs, mental health support and poverty, Grassroots has two regular groups: Baby Roots for young parents and Aspie Roots for young people with Asperger's Syndrome.

I chatted to Lee Wright, one of the early intervention team there about their experiences during Covid-19, the lockdowns and firebreaks they've had in Wales.

The original plan for 2020 had included running food growing workshops, which got cancelled. However, the team, along with the Cardiff Salad Garden project, decided to use the funding to donate plants and seeds to young people, encouraging them to have a go at home, for something to do in the garden with their children. As a result of this project, some of the Baby Roots group appeared on a video with the First Minister for Wales as part of National Allotment Week, talking about how much growing food had helped their sense of wellbeing during lockdown.

> *"When the courgette flower came and then you see a little bit of the courgette, I was made up, it made me feel so good"* Jessica, Baby Roots participant

Another part of this project has been gaining funding to create a wildlife garden. Rather excitingly this will be in a secret garden area next to Cardiff Castle. The space will be used to grow salad and veg, wildlife plants and also to house bird and squirrel feeders. Volunteers to help dig, plant and grow on the plot will include the young people who are part of Grassroots as well as the team there.

Of course, there are so many benefits to this kind of work with people: being outdoors is important for wellbeing, doing the work to dig, sow and plant is good exercise for our bodies, watching plants grow brings a delight and joy that can be hard to come by in challenging times. The opportunity to connect with people outdoors is also crucial to combat loneliness, depression and anxiety, among other things. As 2020 has restricted so much of what they were doing previously, the opportunity to spend time outdoors working hard on allotments or in gardens has been a real positive in amongst all the negative news. The positive impacts of the seemingly mundane is something that shouldn't be lost sight of in the longer term.

Throughout the time, whether restrictions have been tight or more relaxed, Lee and his team have kept in contact with young people via texts, phone calls and social media. You have only to look at their Facebook page to get a good sense of the work being done by the team.

Challenging to Maintain Contact

Maintaining contact has been difficult for many. KPC in Bridgend were also an open access youth provision. Their attendance was around 90 young people per week aged 8 – 18.

They have moved much of their interaction online. This includes posting a Daily Cwtch post to encourage wellbeing and self-care and a Q & A called *Ask A Youth Worker*. In May KPC also got in contact with as many parents of members as they could (the 2020 Annual Report shows they have 326 members). They wanted to see how the families were doing and ask about how they could support them best, were there any issues their children were facing and would the parents were happy for them to engage with their child/ren via phone calls, digital platforms such as Zoom etc. They asked and if the parent would gave consent for this if the child or young person was under 16.

They also sent out postcards to all members giving the different ways in which they could contact KPC - Twitter, Facebook, Instagram, Email etc.

Feedback was positive from parents - they appreciated the call - and KPC were able to gain some feedback on how parents wanted them to engage with them, as well as gaining parental support for the overall project.

As the lockdown lifted the team were able to begin 'catch up' calls with those members they had parental consent to contact. One interesting reflection trend emerged - the uptake was not great. The team member would text first to see when ok to chat but the majority didn't respond and the ones who did weren't used to engaging in this way.

 Many organisations across the board have seen a drop in numbers over Zoom. This seems to point to an additional reluctance for young people to speak on the phone. This is also a long-held reaction of many adults who will often say "I'll respond to text messages but if the phone rings I pretend I'm not here". So it shouldn't be too surprising that this is our young people's reactions as well. Still, it feels like a surprising observation.

I read something about how those of us in our 30's/40's/50's learned how to answer the phone in the hearing of our parents: having to navigate the other parent picking up and how to ask for the person you wanted to speak to. Let me take you back for a moment, to the 1980's and a phone call at 4pm on a school night to my best friend, Lucy:

"Hello Mrs Moulder, can I speak to Lucy please?"

"Yes of course dear, did you not have enough time to chat at school today?"

"Ha ha, not really no!"

"I'll just get her, what about your parents Jenni, how are they?"

"They're fine thank you for asking Mrs Moulder"

All these micro-interactions with other parents taught us how to answer the phone and how to respond to adults asking us questions in a way that today's children do not have to navigate in the era of the personal smart phone. [1].

In August with the change in restrictions, KPC were able to restart face to face outreach work - which was enjoyed by the team, now back via a part time furlough arrangement - and was a way of engaging again with young people they hadn't seen for some time out in the community.

The impact of a lack of contact for both the young people and the youth workers should not be underestimated. This includes physical contact as well as close-quarters contact. The actual outcomes will only really be seen in the medium to long term but threaten to be worse than we might initially anticipated, because of the extended lockdowns and the advent of the highly infectious strains of Covid-19 discovered in the UK in Dec 2020.

> *"I think Covid has been detrimental to us in the support we can give and the type of project we are used to running. ...We anticipate that we will continue to have a disrupted service going forward when future lock-downs etc come into force, but are hoping that we can transition between the actual face to face delivery and our on-line options."*
>
> Alison Mawby, KPC Youth Worker

Continuity of Support for At Risk Young People

In London Juvenis have been operating for the past 5 years "offering bespoke support and training for children and young people involved in or at risk of entering the justice system to turn around their lives and (re)engage with employment, education or training."[2]

They run a series of projects focussed on supporting young people to engage in their community, from working with a fashion retailer to provide suitable attire for young people attending job interviews. They also run the YANA project which supports young people who have been directly affected by gang related violence, sexual grooming, exploitation and domestic violence to recognise and accept their self-worth, build confidence, recognise situations of risk and reduce long term harm.

I spoke to their CEO Winston Goode about the way the pandemic had impacted their work. He told me that their work with young people who have been arrested has not really stopped. The organisation is based in the same building as other youth work organisations, creating a 'youth innovation hub' which looks to offer as much support as possible to young people who engage with Juvenis
.

The example Winston gave me was that of a young person coming into the Juvenis offices, which they were able to keep doing on a one-to-one basis, who might be engaging in self-harming behaviour. They are able to refer that young person to a Psychotherapist who is part of one of the projects they run.

Winston can collect the young person from home, bring him into the Juvenis office on public transport, set up the appointment with the therapist and both before and after that the young man can access the PlayStation and feel like this is his own space for that time.

Collaboration with other members of the innovation hub may not be new thing, but it has definitely been a key feature of Juvenis work during the various restrictions we've all been working under.

Youth Work that asks Questions

Hot Chocolate are a grassroots organisation which grew out of a church-based provision in the centre of Dundee. Their ethos is asking the right questions rather than providing the right answers. Although the physical space they inhabit is within the church, Hot Chocolate is not a traditional church-based youth ministry. As Charis, the Assistant Director explains,

> *"Most cities have a space where the alternative culture young people will hang out so those who dress in black, crazy coloured hair, piercings, weed*

smokers, and in Dundee that is a space called The Grass, which is a big
grassy area in front of the church called The Steeple."

Nearly twenty years ago, the youth worker of the church at the time began by taking cups of hot chocolate out to those hanging out on the green, not with any agenda in mind, but to ask questions and begin to build rapport.

Now, Hot Chocolate works with around 400 young people per year. In pre-covid time this has been through drop-in clubs which are moulded by what the young people want so it's very collaborative, very relational, very fluid and unpredictable. It attracts young people who live in that culture, LGBT young people and those whose self-expression is alternative in style and music. Many of them are struggling with: school, unemployment, criminality or are substances misusers. With Hot Chocolate they report feeling safe, some of them for the first time.

As the first lockdown came into effect, the building had to close which was a huge challenge. Drop in groups moved to online but the aim was to put physical meetings back into the focus. Socially distanced walking one-to-ones with those who were especially vulnerable were one response and another was to place a table outside the front door of their part of the building. A table with a few appropriately distanced chairs under a gazebo meant that some of the team could make contact with young people, handing out the Annual Report, which is a document that the young people them-selves write and illustrate so it's always a big draw for those who belong to Hot Chocolate.

They were also able to signpost young people to what was happening digitally, especially the summer festival, most of which went online. They give out art packs and to begin to ask the quetions again. As a result of the conversations about what the young people miss a guitar was brought out with blankets and anti-bac wipes to make sure that it was as safe an activity as it could be.

Subsequently they have taken groups for day trips using public transport, they have provided safe outdoor spaces for cooking and eating together and have even figured out how they could get the pool table out from inside their building.

Reflections

The work that Juvenis do is targeted and essential. I was impressed that Winston and his team were able to keep going despite the restrictions. It seems to me that if you're working with young people in the criminal justice system there could be catastrophic consequences to stopping this altogether. The fact that they are based in a youth innovation hub is something that intrigued me and made a lot of sense.

We know that young people who are given the tools to thrive will do so. Having some of the most crucial tools like positive community and therapeutic work close to hand can and will make a big difference. I also like the Juvenis approach to online youth work and we'll discuss that further in another chapter.

From targeted intervention work, through to the self-referral and open to everyone type of work that Hot Chocolate run and on into Sidewalk in Scarborough, these are some common threads. The boundaries are fluid, they begin with where the young people are at, thereby not requiring much commitment or imposing the adult agenda. Yet they are centre based and have only begun to do detached work as a result of the pandemic. Both Juvenis and Hot Chocolate offer community, sanctuary and hope to young people whose experiences in life have lacked these. We will look at the importance of each of these in the final chapter.

CHAPTER 5

EMBODIED FAITH - CHRISTIAN YOUTH WORK CHARITY STORIES

Christian Youth Work Charities are organisations whose work has a Christian ethos, but operate separate from any one church or denomination. As might be expected of any youth work provision, their values transcend the framework they are set in and often cross over with other youth work projects and activities. Often they undertake youth work with a strong streak of social justice and the related value of giving worth and dignity to all any human beings.

In this chapter I discovered. from three organisations, just how the pandemic has impacted their work with young people - it's fair to say that it's been a mixed bag. There have been amazing things happening in amongst the challenges brought to all of us by the pandemic and central government response here in the UK.

We'll hear from the Red Balloon Foundation about delivering boxes of essentials and things-to-do and from Urban Devotion about some tentative success with online gaming. Worth Unlimited told me about the challenges presented by contacting young people who had no personal, private space at home and about wellbeing package deliveries growing in number across the estate.

Some of those I spoke to told me about experiencing disorientation and real difficulties in making decisions in the initial days of the lockdown in March 2020. Others talk about maintaining a frenetic pace of activity which saw them working on Good Friday for the first time or hosting big online events like the Scripture Union Boost conference.

The importance of boxes!

Let's begin with the Red Balloon Foundation working in in Essex and other locations nearby, I spoke to Lizzie Lysaght, their Partnerships Manager who described the work they do as 'creating scaffolding for youth work projects'.

They have a large team of 25 people many of whom were furloughed in first lockdown. During this time, they operated with 8 workers including the person who was managing the operations. As the first lockdown was announced the team realised that the young people would need them more rather than less. I think this has been a thread running through everything I've heard about in writing this book - the realisation for every organisation that young people were going to need more support rather than less as this challenging time kicked off.

For the Foundation, the children's groups went virtual over Zoom – along with the accompanying question of how do the games translate? Lizzie's reflection was that the team were surprised at how well the majority of them did work in the online context, I know that this has not necessarily been the experience of everyone!

One of the strands of the Foundation is to support Sunday School in different churches, providing one team member per church to support this. When the first lockdown was brought in, Sunday mornings became Zoom calls with groups of young people and children, using the usual teams of people to send a box out beforehand for the activities. This worked very well indeed, with team members seeing each other more often, and more children and young people on the call. They found that more families engaged than would have if they had to get to churches.

For the interim period, these groups went into bubbles of 15 in church halls which are often big enough to socially distance. As far as the children were concerned, the provision was consistent. The Foundation find that the last, the least and the lost come and these children need to know that the people who they trust will still be there.

In the week before the first lockdown the Foundation was due to launch a lunch club on a TLG[1] model for the 'just about managing' families. This was quickly re-envisioned as weekly boxes of food and personalised educational activities for children delivered to families by volunteers. The boxes were tailored for each family. There was one family who'd just had a baby and they got a box with formula and other essentials for a new baby. The Foundation are still doing these box deliveries for the whole Epping district and beyond.

"In many cases this has been led by the young people who have wanted to do something to meet a need that they see around them" Lizzie Lysaght, The Red Balloon Foundation

Boxes are a big theme for the Foundation, not only do they deliver food and educational materials but also the Sunday and Midweek Club boxes. These are posted to the children and they have to guess how the enclosed materials will be used in the group meeting, which happens over Zoom. It's a huge undertaking but one that has seen the engagement of young people, children and whole families increase at a time when many others are watching numbers fall away.

Wellbeing packages

Listen Threads is a small young people led social enterprise that makes, prints and sells clothing and accessories in Birmingham. It is a project connected to Worth Unlimited. Both Listen Threads and Worth Unlimited work with an Asset Based Community Development approach, which, as we have discussed previously, is a particular view of community building that focusses on using the assets already present in the community rather than a deficit model which would look to meet needs of the community, perceived or actual.

Listen Threads was co-founded by Janey Barrett and Chloe Latham, who is 24 years old. The group of young women were asked what do they already have a passion for, and the answer was fashion. They are now used to meeting up every week and getting on with the work of making or printing, parcelling up and sending out orders.

Case Study: Young Leaders

The March lockdown affected Listen Threads, in that meeting up was no longer possible and they had a period of time where the only contact was through doorstep delivery of wellbeing packages by Janey, the youth worker. This began with dropping off 8 packages in the week and grew as they became aware of more isolated young women in their community. Now Janey delivers 30 packages a week and Chloe says :

> *"It's just lovely to know that someone is thinking about me in that moment. Janey is great at keeping in contact like this, it means a lot to us who are receiving the packages."*

In the summer they met in person again, an activity classed as support for vulnerable young people, as each member of the group has mental health challenges. The original group is for 18 + and meets during the day, but Chloe is keen to begin an after-school group for those who'd like to and are comfortable to come out. The building they meet in is small and they only have it for a couple of hours at a time. Keeping the group small will be really valuable as small numbers means everyone gets to talk to one another, which is an important part of building the community of Listen Threads.

Chloe has been part of the Worth Unlimited community local to her since she was 14, she is passionate about the role that Worth and Janey have played in her life. Chloe had the vision of setting up the girls' groups, where she believes she can be a role model because she has faced many similar difficulties to those the 12 – 16's group are facing now. She sees herself as the 'cool older Auntie'.

"I was *youthworked*" says Chloe in her broad Brummie accent, "I know how important it was for me so I want to give that same [experience] to other girls too"

Chloe is a clear picture of the essential role that youth work and the youth worker plays in the lives of young people. She speaks with great self-assurance about her role in Listen Threads and how much Janey and the project have impacted her own journey towards becoming a more confident person.

Michelin Meals and Family Feasts

Urban Devotion are another Birmingham asset-based community development organisation. Prior to lockdown, their CEO Andy Winmill had been developing a relationship with the organisation that became the lead food provider for the city. From Mon 23rd March to end of July, Urban Devotion were delivering around 90 meals every day. Included was a Michelin starred restaurant who ran a 'sponsored' programme which was *meals on wheels* and also offering a meal to a needy family for every restaurant meal purchased.

Urban Devotion were seen as an essential service, involved in doorstep deliveries and checking in on people, which meant they had contact with more people. In July they adapted their practice of regular 'Family Feast' evenings to become their main food delivery point. Family Feasts are takeaways, for families to pick up - and as a result, continue to build the connections made in the first few weeks of lockdown.

Drop in clubs have been replaced this year by pop-up activities that could be run in flexible ways ensuring that further restrictions wouldn't stop them. This is another thread that runs through many of the organisations I've spoken to, especially those with a self-reflective streak. Stopping activities that have been part of the long-term programme of the organisation is a hard choice. Leaders have reflected with me that this has been painful, but necessary, and that good can already be seen in the decision.

As Urban Devotion were able to open up buildings again, they put on sessions called 'Check-Ins' inviting young people to come and see them. These formed an effective 'triage' with young people, because how can young people be supported unless they are known and seen by the team.

Andy has a significant presence in the local secondary school, which was once the second worst school in England and Wales, becoming an Ambassador (a governance role) for the Academy. The school and Urban Devotion have worked in partnership to welcome kids back to school in September 2020 and the team are in the school 5 days a week, offering mentoring and small group work. For many of the local community kids, school is the only safe and consistent space in their week.

It was very disorientating

This kind of commitment to young people and the relationships that have been built over time is echoed by the Worth Unlimited Mobile Youth Bus project in Waltham Forest (London). Their manager Helen Perry and I had a conversation which was very reflective in nature, something I think is going to become even more important to youth work as we begin to look beyond this covid era. We will explore this further in the final chapter of the book.

Helen manages a team made up of employed staff, sessional workers and volunteers and was candid enough with me to say that she found the initial experience of lockdown very disorientating indeed. Questions of how to make decisions about keeping staff and young people safe, how to stay in touch with young people when the majority of contact pre-covid was open access and mobile. They had been taking the bus into 5 different boroughs, meaning there were very few details kept about who had been accessing the support, which in turn meant that making contact with young people themselves was difficult and parental contact even harder.

Worth Unlimited's senior team quickly arranged to put on online training sessions during the first lockdown. This was not only an opportunity to do some training that there hadn't been time to do previously, but also meant that staff teams were meeting up together much more often than usual.

In Waltham Forest, Helen acknowledges that these were testing times for managers, making difficult decisions based either on very little knowledge about the levels of risk (as the message had been simplified down to 'Stay at Home Save Lives' there seemed to be no room for nuanced approach in the first lockdown). But they were also working with very little specific guidance in those first few weeks.

There were some online Zoom groups set up which had a mixed response and success. Like so many other projects, it worked for those young people who engaged but not for others. During that first lockdown period, Helen's team kept in contact with all those young people they had contact details for, offering mentoring sessions online or over the telephone. This was a challenge for those young people who did not have any private personal space at home, as they were sharing a bedroom with siblings and all other living spaces were also being shared with family members who were all at home.

As restrictions eased, the Worth Unlimited team went 'detached' and had good contact with young people over the summer months. They also sent out activity packs to those young people who were not appearing in parks or on the streets. Since schools returned the numbers of young people out and about dropped. Helen's team had planned to return to the community centre where they had previously had a regular presence, to run a music project with smaller numbers and perhaps offer some football or other sport in the outdoor areas of that centre. The idea was to begin small and add other activity focussed groups as and when was possible. But then the November lockdown happened so those went on hold.

Reflections

Helen's reflections on her experiences as a team manager are about the shock of the speed of the lockdown and the pressure to be creative in the midst of very challenging circumstances. She talks about that pressure being eased by talking to others in similar roles, who understood the nature of the challenge in youth work, who could help her release the fear she had about making decisions on behalf of other people. The team have been able to concentrate on keeping in contact, and being present for as many of their young people as possible.

As a contrast to the approach of Worth Unlimited, the key to Urban Devotion's approach has been about flexibility and adaptations, ensuring that any new elements of work were 'future proofed', meaning that they could continue throughout further changes to restrictions. The continued presence in schools from when they reopened to the whole community is very encouraging to hear about, especially at a time when many schools have closed their doors to visitors of any kind, even parents.

Listen Threads is youth work through an enterprise lens and I was really inspired by the conversation I had with Janey and Chloe. Although the actual making of clothing and accessories has only continued through the pandemic because Janey has carried on, it is clear that this enterprise has had a big impact not only on Chloe but the others in that group. Janey's commitment to maintaining the connection in person has meant a great deal.

I'm encouraged to hear that Zoom has worked so well for the Red Balloon Foundation in contrast to others who have found it a challenge. I think online youth work has become an approach to youth work that needs its own set of stories and reflections so we'll talk some more about this in another chapter. It's clear that delivering boxes has become a key element to their work. What a great testament that is to all those who volunteer their time and energy to ensure that the relationships are maintained through the provision of food, other non-food essentials as well as activities for the whole family.

Constant Belief

Each of these organisations has responded to the crisis created by the Covid-19 pandemic by finding creative ways to keep in contact with the young people who were part of their organisations and have often ended up supporting more than just those! Covid has had a significant impact on the projects or programmes run in each case, with the understanding that youth work is far more about the relationships, than it is about the programmes really coming to the fore. It was Chloe Latham from Listen Threads who really summed that up for me when she said,

> *"I know that youth work works because of the impact it's had on me. I would never have done what I've achieved if not for Janey and her constant belief in me"*

CHAPTER 6

NEW ADVENTURES - OUTDOOR YOUTH WORK

In the midst of this pandemic, detached or street-based and outdoor youth work have been the consistent presence, permitted even in the toughest of restricted times. Many of the organisations I have spoken to mentioned keeping activities outside, particularly as the first lockdown lifted and we were able to meet, socially distanced, outdoors.

The weather in the summer of 2020 really enabled this to happen week after week. There haven't been many summers in living memory that have been as consistently dry and warm. We looked at organisations doing detached or street based work in an earlier chapter, so here we will turn our attention to those working with young people in the outdoors.

Most commonly this is uniformed organisations. In the UK this covers a broad range of organisations from the Scouting and Guiding movements, the Boys and Girls Brigade and the many Cadet corps which young people join in great numbers. I discovered in the course of writing this book that many of the Fire Services around the country have either a cadet type of programme or intervention type of youth work. We'll find out more about that in this chapter. We'll also learn about the work of The Outward Bound Trust who have a mission to inspire young people through experiencing the outdoors in ways which challenge and build resilience.

The Scouting Movement

There has been an influx of numbers joining the Scouts in particular since 2007, when the boys-only rule was dropped.[1] The majority of the new joiners are girls, keen to learn skills like rifle shooting, trekking, outdoor camping as well as the social justice oriented badges related to homelessness awareness, mental health and climate change. The Scouting movement has not been without its controversies over its 112 year history, however Scouts continue to adapt and change their practices in order to remain open and welcome to boys and girls across a diverse range of their communities. One very interesting comment I came across was from a new Scout leader in Blackburn who is reported in The Guardian as saying:

> *"Teachers tell us it's really obvious which children go to scouts because they're more independent and very good at problem solving." Nisbah Hussain, Scout Leader, Brookhouse Primary School, Blackburn*[2]

The Great Indoors

Early on in the pandemic chief scout Bear Grylls launched the Great Indoors initiative with the Scouts movement, involving 100 activities to help occupy young people's minds. These have included:

- writing a postcard to your future self
- creating a tornado in a jar using water, sand and washing up liquid
- creating a fancy frame for a photograph you love

- and keeping a diary including writing down good things
that have happened however small.

The Scouts have been busy setting up events where those in the national leadership are able to share good practice and encourage scout leaders from all over the country to be creative about how they engage their scout groups. One of them was a virtual craft session, making a 'talking stick', which would usually have been used in a scouts session to facilitate conversations but were now being used around the dinner table to facilitate family discussion.

Another group, Biggleswade District Scouts, had set up a video of 19 different challenges that the scouts could do at home, themed around the badges that Scouts can earn. It's a great resource for anyone with kids at home to use – available on Youtube[3].

Scout troops have also been encouraged to pair up with care homes in an attempt to bring some cheer to both the recipients and the givers of letters and cards with a teabag. Intergenerational connections are really important for both of the generations involved; if ever you've watched 'Old People's Home for 4 year olds' you'll have seen this at work. Indeed this is one of the joys of being part of a church community where children and the elderly are able to co-mingle and enjoy each other's presence. I'm impressed by the way that Scouts are so often looking out for others, even those who are not their peers.

> *"Pictures and letters have been cheering up my Nanna and Grandad while I can't see them to give them a hug, I wanted to start doing the same for other people."*

[4] says James…, a six year old beaver scout in Enfield, north London

Both Scout leaders I spoke to told me about switching to Zoom and trying to encourage the children to keep active with scavenger hunts and mini Olympics type of activities. Jen, Cub Scout leader, describes the overall feeling that if Cubs were happy and smiling at the end of any Zoom session then this was counted as a win.

With the switch to online sessions has come the need for different behaviour management skills, which I think reflects the picture across all youth activities online. A new etiquette is needed, teaching young people new ways of connecting with others that looks very different to the noisy, chaotic beginning to any face-to-face meetings. Paul, a volunteer Scout Leader in South Croydon told me that returning to face to face meeting in September was refreshing for both leaders and members after 5 months of online only meetings. Jen's group have not gone back to face to face due to her proximity to a medically vulnerable person, this has been a factor elsewhere in our discussions, though I'd suggest not as much as might be expected.

Dream Big At Home

Woodcraft Folk have been around since 1925 when there was a break away from the scouting movement. The Woodcraft Folk have a strong emphasis on co-operation and co-operative living as opposed to what was seen as the more 'militaristic' approach of the scouts. They also permitted both girls and boys to join, which was fairly radical at the time. The term 'woodcraft' refers more to the skills of living in the open air than making things out of wood and their overall ethos includes understanding of important issues like the environment, world debt and global conflict.They seek to develop activities focussing on sustainable development; and encourage children to think, hoping that they will in turn help build a peaceful, fairer world.[5]

What impressed me most in the conversation I had with one of their leaders in the South East was this focus that online groups have on issues of justice including refugees and asylum and climate emergency. The latter is the aim of their #DreamBigAtHome campaign supported by the national Woodcraft Folk organisation. On their website it states:

> *"Our normal Woodcraft Folk youth activities can't happen during lockdown, but the fun can continue at home. Our work is more important than ever – linking up young people, playing games, making friends and continuing a sense of community and connection while we are physically apart."*[6]

There is a wealth of links to activities and actions for young people to get involved in on the website, from the weekly challenges, to anti-racist education, climate emergency and an archive. The Woodcraft Folk don't necessarily get headlines in the way the Scouting movement do, but they are diligent, creative and caring in their understanding of young people and children, encouraging all members to care for themselves, for others and for the world around them.

In-School Adventure Days

The Outward Bound Trust have been a presence in residential youth work since 1941 when their first centre opened in Aberdovey, Wales. They have grown into one of the biggest educational charities, helping young people to defy limitations, equipping them with a stronger sense of self-belief, the ability to cope better with stressful situations and interact more positively with others. I spoke to Natalie Harling, who is the Director of Business Development. I was really interested to hear her talk about working with young people in terms which are really recognisable to anyone working in youth work. She spoke of the value of residential work with young people, taking them away from their usual surroundings and introducing them to challenging circumstances, as well as the need to create space for young people to decompress and to clear their heads as well as to learn new skills.

I particularly liked the way she talked about the need to act now, not to wait for life to 'return to normal'. I've tried, with this book, to show that youth work is still happening during this Covid-19 era, during some of the most restrictive of times we have known in the UK for a generation. Thereby demonstrating the creativity and tenacity of youth workers in so many contexts to keep on connecting with and building relationships with young people. We'll look at this a bit more in the final chapter, but I hope you've seen that amongst the hard work needed to 'pivot' into new activities, a new way of working, there is hope, stability and community being built even during this challenging times.

The Outward Bound Trust have also had to shift their work, quite dramatically. They've furloughed staff who would normally be involved in regular 5-day residential programmes throughout the year, taking children and young people from urban environments into the wild. They've had to think creatively about how to keep on engaging and do so in a way that supports not only the young people themselves but also their communities.

Since September 2020, they've been running In-School Adventure Days. These take place in schools in the locality of one or other of their 6 centres in Snowdonia, the Lake District and the Highlands and have been incredibly well received by children and the school staff. They also, in partnership with the CPRE countryside charity, have been lobbying governments to increase people's access to countryside, emphasising how essential these places and spaces are for our mental health. They believe that opportunities for young people getting outdoors and connecting with others safely are urgently needed to avoid the prolonging of a crisis which will already define this generation.

Their In-School Adventure Days have been the start of this, demonstrating the joy and confidence that can be found in outdoor environments, even when that is the school field or woodland in the locality. Children who have been struggling with the anxiety of going outside during a time when we are repeatedly being told to stay at home and not mix with others, have reported feeling more confident and enthusiastic about the outdoors. It's really heart-warming to hear as are the reports from the school staff,

> "They come in smiling; they look forward to the next session, they're doing things like 'life skills' that they maybe haven't had the opportunity to do before, they're motivated and happy and that's what we're aiming for." Katie Chappell, Headteacher, Shap Primary School[7]

> "One of the main [benefits] has been the teachers' confidence for outdoor learning. I've been teaching for nearly 20 years and I'm outdoorsy but even myself, just taking that class out [is challenging], especially if you've got pupils who are tricky... I think it's a bit of a legacy – once the instructors go, they're going to have empowered a whole cohort of staff at our school...which I think is huge"[8] Siobhan Bradley, Deputy Headteacher, Lundavra Primary School

Combining Outdoor Activity with Safety

I put out a plea on Facebook for people who were involved in youth work to get in touch and I had a lot of responses, which was fantastic. Possibly the most surprising of those however was the West Yorkshire Fire and Rescue Service (WYFRS): Youth Interventions team. Charlie talked to me with amazing enthusiasm about the work that they do with targeted young people, some of it in partnership with the Princes Trust, to build awareness and resilience as well as teaching about the potential impact of anti-social behaviours like fire setting.

This is targeted intervention youth work, similar in approach to the work of Juvenis which we heard about in a previous chapter. They run programmes which target young people from schools, colleges, pupil referral units and the local young offending team, who are at risk of anti-social behaviour. However, I've included it in this chapter because of the similar use of challenging situations, but in natural surroundings to build resilience and confidence in young people. The young people take part in Drill Square activities alongside the Youth Interventions team and also members of the WYFRS. They are challenged to scale ladders, to use the water hoses and other related outdoor activities, (fully supervised of course).

The Youth Interventions team have also got a partnership with the Princes Trust and run their courses as well. During the pandemic this has been online, with WYFRS being the only fire service to be running this type of programme digitally. The outcomes have been better than expected and I think this is down to the creativity and drive of the team of youth workers.

There is a lot of work that goes into re-shaping these courses for online delivery, ensuring that the experience is engaging for the young people and not just running them as they would in-person. It's clear that this has made a difference. Over the summer of 2020 they had nine young people on their Fire Setters course digitally. They attended 3 sessions a day over the course of 6 weeks. The Youth team were concerned that it might not work well but have found that it did. The nine young people bonded as a group and had high levels of engagement. The real plus points were that being able to join a group from their own home, really helped with social anxieties and cut down on the amount of time travelling! One participant lived in another part of the county and would have had to take two busses to get to the Fire Station, the fact that they could join from their own room was a huge bonus.

The Youth team are now busy planning the next couple of courses they'll be offering to young people and are now being asked by other fire services for advice about running courses digitally.

The Importance of Outdoors

As we find ourselves in the middle of the third lockdown in England, in the darkest, coldest, wettest part of the year, it's harder to muster up the energy to get outdoors, let alone encouraging our teenagers to do it. My own children are reluctant, and I am concerned. They used to get a reasonable amount of exercise or at least time outside, on the way to and from school, during PE lessons and at break times. Now it's almost impossible to get them to scoot around the block. There are a few factors at play here but my concern is that they will lose all fitness, that they will find it so hard to get back into cycling to school or playing tennis or football or even just being outdoors down at the local park.

It is difficult to overstate how important it is that we encourage our young people and children to get outdoors regularly, youth workers need to be working outdoors to build confidence as well as fitness levels. There are lots of organisations doing this already, let's see more taking a lead from them. We'll talk a little more about this in the final chapter as I believe this is a crucial element to where we must go from here.

CHAPTER 7

TO ZOOM OR NOT TO ZOOM? - ONLINE YOUTH WORK

In 1998 Youthwork magazine had a slightly tongue in cheek column called 'Adventures of an On Line Youth Worker' which was written by Nick Page, master of youth work comedy. The column consisted of emails written by youth workers and was a play on the initials AOL, recognisable to many of us as a pioneer of the early days of the internet, providing dial-up internet in the 1990's.

By 1997 AOL was the world's largest email provider with around nine million subscribers[1]. They still exist today but in a much reduced form, having found themselves on the wrong side of technology as broadband came into being. The column has long been retired but can still be found in print copies of previous editions of the magazine.

In 2020 we have seen a massive increase in 'online youth work' across a variety of platforms. In April 2020 a Facebook group called 'Digital Youth Work' was set up and in October 2020 Tim Gough's Grove Booklet called 'Youth Ministry Online: using social media platforms to connect with teenagers' was published. A number of those I spoke to had made online provision a key part of their strategy and, as with the rest of society, are planning to keep some of the online work going, even when we can gather together in the same physical spaces.

As has been noted elsewhere in this book, the reactions of young people to the use of Zoom have been varied. Largely, young people have eschewed it, especially after the first few times where it was novel to do and meant they could see their friends from their usual groups at a time when they weren't seeing any friends at all. I think a note of caution should be sounded, not only for young people but for society as a whole, around the potential for virtual connections to replace physical presence. Being in the same space, at the same time, being able to hug or hold hands or in some way make a physical connection with another human being is vital. There is a wealth of evidence that shows just how important physical proximity is to human beings[2].

However, in a time when physically gathering, in the same space at the same time is severely curtailed, the virtual or online spaces have become even more important as a means to either make contact with or convey information to people and youth work is no different.

Zoom

The video conference calling platform gained a sudden and meteoric rise in popularity at the beginning of the first lockdown. The CEO of Zoom has found himself in the centre of one of the most rapid periods of change in modern history. Initially developed as a tool for business, reporting user figures of 10 million in December 2019, in April 2020 that figure jumped to 300 million. If it felt like everyone was on Zoom, it's because they were![3]

It is a platform that has become important for education, for socialising and even for worship, weddings and funerals. They have worked hard at adding new features, addressing security concerns and employing a bigger customer services department as the lockdown continued. Anyone who has used Zoom for working, in fact using any video conference calling platform, will have experienced 'Zoom fatigue'. It has become apparent that meeting over video call is more tiring than meeting in person. This is attributed to the different level of attention required, and also to the lack of eye contact, making us feel disconnected despite the face-to-face feel of the connection.

Zoom is the platform of choice for millions of adults working from home, and along with Google's Meet and Microsoft's Teams, has also been the platform used by schools to provide online learning. There were problems with security in the early weeks of the coronavirus restrictions, these have largely been overcome thanks to Zoom's response to 'react fast and hide nothing'. They dedicated themselves to addressing bugs and hiring new staff to ensure they were getting it right[4].

Zoom has been mentioned in nearly all my conversations with youth workers as it represents a significant portion of their youth work in the last year. One particularly interesting discussion about the use of Zoom was with Andy from Urban Devotion. He had noticed that children and young people really seem to have rejected the idea of video calling. In the context of his work, he was finding that families may not have access to internet at home, and they were not familiar with video conference calling. Which is unsurprising given that even Eric Yuan, the CEO of Zoom himself, had never contemplated the platform being used for anything other than a business application. For the most part the families Andy was in contact with requested the use of WhatsApp or Instagram, rather than Zoom, Teams or even Facebook. Andy said:

"We already know that young people mostly don't use Facebook, they are much more likely to be on Instagram, Snap Chat and the new platforms that adults don't know much about yet. If we as adults want to engage with

young people online, we cannot assume they will want to do it the way we want them to."

I would add a counterpoint to this, because although Andy's point is a good one, there is always more than one way to look at these things. The Red Balloon Foundation find that their young people really engaged well with Zoom, enjoying the socialising as well as the opportunity to learn. The West Yorkshire Fire and Rescue Service also found that the young people who attended their Fire Setters course and the Princes Trust programmes through Zoom really took to not only the learning elements but also the group bonding which is so key to these programmes.

A group of nine young people who had never met before in real life, bonded well over Zoom. The key here I think was the regularity of these meetings. The time commitment for the young people is huge, they are required to show up online three times a day for an hour and a half per session, for 6 weeks. But in that time, friendships can be built. This is the beauty of youth work, and it can work, even over Zoom.

Instagram

Instagram is where the young people are, having rolled out new features like IGTV, Instagram Live and Stories (a feature that is spreading, first to Facebook and then, more surprisingly, to Twitter with the name 'Fleets'). Their most recent innovation is Instagram's answer to TikTok: Reels. Whether you understand all that language or not, Instagram is one of the biggest social media platforms, and the one favoured by many young people. It is the platform which has the greatest potential to influence young people, and influence is the name of the game.

Even before Covid-19 even existed, Instagram was curating and shaping our young people's lives through celebrity endorsements of anything and everything, and also through those who achieve celebrity status because they are influential on social media. An influencer is someone who shares fun, aspirational, comedic or life-style content, engaging with fans and followers online[5]. You'll find influencers on Instagram, and also on YouTube. There are lots of youth work organisations on Instagram, using Live sessions to encourage young people, to engage them in a task for the week, or enter a challenge set by the youth worker.

There are daily video posts about inspirational thoughts or moti-vating ideas, fun challenges or fascinating work being done. Insta-gram is an excellent platform for curating content and engaging young people and is used by KPC youth, Grassroots Cardiff, Urban Devotion, Worth Unlimited and Listen Threads, plus many more.

One of the stories I heard about the use of Instagram by a youth organisation was from when Covid-19 restrictions were first intro-duced. Lee and the team at Grassroots teamed up with the Youth Service in Wales and began producing video content for their social media channels, this included 'story time' videos for the children of the Baby Roots group and cooking videos. Their partnership with a supermarket locally meant they could deliver food parcels and include recipe cards in order to support the young people they were delivering to. This is a very creative way to use Instagram and other video viewing platforms to support good youth work.: videos that show young people how to use the ingredients they've just been handed, or videos which help young parents with their baby's bedtime routine.

YouTube

In my own home, YouTube is the most used social media platform. I know I know, if you're over a certain age then YouTube is for music videos and funny videos of laughing babies and cute puppies or kittens. But for my two boys, aged 11 and 15, YouTube is their hanging out space, along with Minecraft and Roblox (both of which they play socially – more about young people playing online games with youth workers in a bit). They watch hours and hours of other people playing games like Fortnite, Among Us, Minecraft and Roblox. They have conversations about these videos and the gamers who play them, talking about Preston or DanTDM and the like as if they know them personally. It's baffling as their parent but intriguing as a youth worker!

Since the start of the pandemic, Youtube has of course been used by churches, youth groups and other organisations to get their message out. Many churches now have their own YouTube channel and have become more proficient in creating content that is attractive. Because of YouTube some churches in the UK have seen 'attendance' figures rise as more people than their congregation numbers have watched services. YouTube has literally put the creation of good quality video content into the hands of the masses.

Of course, not everything on YouTube is good quality, either in content or in presentation but it has provided a way for people to reach out to others. It is a medium for people to continue to enjoy church activities, and also a medium for youth organisations to send out messages, to provide training, to hold conversations on different themes for young people, and well, anyone really to watch.

That being said, whilst there are a number of different youth organisations on YouTube, not many of those I spoke to have used YouTube in the past year. Much of what can be found on this platform is from the US, or is videos such as 'Youth Group Game Ideas for Zoom' - so not young people focussed and more of a resourcing usage.

Facebook Lives

Facebook first began their world takeover in the early 2000's, starting as a network for college students and quickly becoming the leader in the social media world. Facebook now boasts 2.7 billion active users, having passed the one billion mark in 2012, the first social network to do so. WhatsApp, Instagram and Messenger are all owned by Facebook, so those statistics rise further to 3.14 billion users of at least one of these platforms each month[6].

Historically Facebook has not been the best social media platform for businesses or churches, even now the algorithm that is used to curate our timelines means that it can be hard work for businesses to be visible. However, Facebook Live, with its ability to stream live content and have people interact by typing comments whilst watching, has given youth workers, churches and other organisations a good platform to connect with Facebook users, and there are a lot of them!

A number of the organisations I spoke to have got good Facebook pages with interesting content and good interaction with their audience. Grassroots and MINE youth were two that particularly stood out.

WhatsApp

One youth worker recorded this reflection on support via text:

> *"I text open ended questions, I wait, 7 minutes pass, no response, I send a summary of where we got to last week and I get a reply. I have not done text support before, so every text I send and the response I receive is a moment of reflection, how could I have worded this differently or created a more engaging space. I decide to ask her if there's anything she wants to talk about?"*[7]

During that first lockdown period, Helen's team at Worth Unlimited Waltham Forest, used WhatsApp to keep in contact with all those young people they had contact details for, offering mentoring sessions online or over the telephone. This was a challenge for those young people who did not have any private, personal space at home, sharing a bedroom with siblings and all the other living spaces being shared with family members who were all at home. But the team were able to keep the contact going using WhatsApp and this has resulted in stronger connections with young people.

Gaming and mentoring

Case Study: Gaming & Mentoring

At Urban Devotion in Birmingham, there is one lad they have contact with who is a county lines concern. He was regularly knocking on the door, wanting to know when activities would be starting up. The team offered him online mentoring, which he refused. Someone had an idea to offer interaction through online gaming. Now this lad logs onto gaming sessions with the Urban Devotion team weekly. The young person teaches the adults in the team how to play the game (age appropriate) and also engages with conversations around mental health and wellbeing. The key is that the team entered his space as apprentices (or noobs as the gaming terminology goes) and needed teaching about his world, which totally changed the dynamic of the relationships that might have been there in the mentoring space.

The first time I heard about using gaming for a youth group was while listening to a conversation broadcast on You Tube between youth workers for the Diocese of London. The youth worker for Holy Trinity Brompton, Tom Clark talked about a boy from Hungary joining in with their gaming group. The discussion that followed threw up questions of proximity and relationship: can youth work be meaningful at such a distance? How do relationships work when they are exclusively online?

Juvenis, London have been using online gaming as a tool for keeping in contact with their young people during the pandemic. Winston's team have been less tentative with this than others I've spoken to. He takes the view that conversation whilst playing FIFA or other games online is the same as a conversation that might take place whilst playing table tennis in another context. They have drawn up risk assessments and encourage their staff to keep these conversations light, if the young person wants to talk about serious or complex stuff then they are encouraged to do that in a face-to-face meeting at the Juvenis offices. Maintaining contact with vulnerable young people has been the driving force behind their work during the pandemic.

I think there seems to be a reluctance in youth ministry circles especially about using these games to connect with young people. This might be due to an inherent distrust of games and online gaming platforms, which may itself stem from the notion that games take away time that the young person might be connecting with friends, family and the youth ministry programme. I think this point of view is changing and it may be changing more quickly because of the pandemic. Families with much more time together now are more likely to play games together, there are more consoles and accessories being sold that enable this.

When it doesn't go so well

KPC, Bridgend had moved much of their interaction into the online space, especially Instagram and Facebook, including posting a Daily Cwtch post to encourage wellbeing and self-care and then also Ask A Youth Worker. However, the digital engagement numbers have continued to be low and invariably the same young people. This has been challenging and has not reached those who may be harder to engage.

There's a similar story for Loyd at the Rudgwick Youth Centre and in other contexts. I think this is a picture replicated for many, The challenges of limited face-to-face, in real life connection has presented challenges which few in the youth work world have experienced before the implementation of Covid-19 restrictions. As we are now in the third lockdown, this time with many young people being taught online, even if they are in a school setting, their willingness to engage in a group session over Zoom or similar video conference platform is low after having spent so much of the school day plugged into lessons online. Our young people are exhausted, missing their friends, missing the routine that going to school brings them and anxious about what their future holds. One more Zoom is not going to engage them.

Fortunately, we have seen that there are many different ways to engage young people online, so perhaps what's needed is a little more creative thought about how we might engage young people in this space – not only which platform to use but also who is creating the content. Is it us as adults creating for the young people or could the young people create for themselves and their peers? I have a feeling that the young people would outstrip the adults on this one!

Reflections

Having had to move into the realm of online youth work suddenly, and without perhaps too much opportunity to do a lot of the ground work, we are still at the beginning of this journey. From Bible Studies for faith-based groups, through to advice and information about mental health or wellbeing and on to mentoring through gaming or even via text, there are as many different ways for youth work to be online as there are many different ways to do youth work in person. This is going to be a large part of how we maintain contact with, and indeed build relationships with young people and so it's worth getting to grips with your risk assessments and your policies about using social media or video conference platforms.

I'm aware that one of the biggest social media platforms I haven't mentioned is TikTok, this is because none of the youth workers I have spoken to mentioned it as a platform they were using. That's not to say that it cannot be used by youth workers to make contact with and build relationships with young people. Tim Gough's Grove Booklet[8] has some good tips about TikTok and how to use it for youth work, it's written from a faith-based perspective but has some good advice for all those working with young people.

CHAPTER 8

WHERE DO WE GO FROM HERE?

Having taken you on a whistle stop tour of youth work practice in the time since March 2020, we now turn our attention to the future, perhaps most specifically the immediate future. As the Covid-19 crisis continues to impact our daily lives here in the UK it is difficult to predict what will happen in the next six months.

However, it becomes all the more necessary to consider how to emerge from crisis mode and what kind of a world do we want to build in the aftermath of this? Our young people and children have been among the unhappiest in Europe since the mid 2000's[1]. We cannot kid ourselves that the latest crisis was the start of this. However it might present an opportunity to make radical changes in a short time.

In an article for the Infed website, Mark Smith calls for changes that will stick[2], in schools and in informal settings like youth work. It's important to look deeper, past the surface 'normal' that involves wearing face masks and keeping your distance from other human beings. Although these things will have a long lasting impact, we need to give some more in depth consideration to this question about the kind of world we want to rebuild.

Hopefully you've seen as we've gone through this book that I feel particularly strongly about an asset-based approach to youth and community development. It's an approach that can work in most of the contexts we've heard from. So, as we consider the future and a way forward that is not simply responding to what's happening in our world but actively building communities which will be resilient against the storms that are yet to come, let us look at the opportunities through the lens of the asset-based approach[3].

Stability

Every single person I have spoken to in the writing of this book has talked in terms of providing stability and consistency in the lives of the young people in their community. Stability in the form of presence, even when it's very different from the kind of presence we were used to, is an asset to the youth work community. One of the strengths of current youth work practice is the determination of youth workers to offer stability in a very uncertain world.

Stability looks like showing up: it looks like maintaining contact through almost impossible circumstances; it looks like wellbeing packages, giving out seeds, doorstep deliveries of food and craft resources; it looks like teams of people changing how they work in a matter of days or weeks in order to carry on delivering their vision of encouraging thriving and flourishing in our young people's lives. These people are a huge asset to their community, bringing the people whose lives they touch from isolation into community.

Young People are an Amazing Force for Good

Young people are their own biggest asset.As youth workers we know this but it can be hard for them to see it themselves. One of the key values for the National Youth Agency and for youth work as a whole discipline is that youth work is transformational in its nature, that the voices of young people are amplified in order to develop their place in society as a whole.

Chloe Latham from Listen Threads is a fantastic example of this. Without the presence of youth work giving her a voice, she would not be the person she is today. Without the presence of youth work and youth workers, a 10 year old Marcus Rashford might never have risen to the top flight of English football. He might never have had the opportunity to influence the UK government to provide meals for children who would otherwise go hungry during school holidays and also be the catalyst for the big fashion brand Burberry donating significant sums of money to youth projects in some of the poorest areas of the UK[4]. His own commitment to amplify the voices of the vulnerable is astonishing, in his own words,

"These children matter. These children are the future of this country. They are not just another statistic. And for as long as they don't have a voice, they will have mine"[5]

At the time of writing, Marcus is 23 years old, meaning that he is still in the young person age bracket according to the NYA's definition. There are many other teenagers who have helped shape our world, Malala, Greta Thunberg, Thandiwe Abdullah. The latter might not be a household name here in the UK. But at 17 she is a co-founder of the Black Lives Matter LA Youth Vanguard and Time Magazine named her as one of the most influential teenagers in 2018. Abdullah has become one of her generation's most powerful voices on issues relating to social justice[6]. Young people's voices are powerful and effect change, our work with them should be youth-led and not adult dictated.

Sanctuary, Community and Hope

Out of all these crises and more, we need to rebuild a world around sanctuary, community and hope[7]. Our young people and children need to see change and change that is positive, not a wholescale change to a high-tech, no-touch future[8] which will only benefit the high-tech corporations. Yes, online learning is probably here to stay, yes online contact will continue in some contexts. But being physically present in a shared space that does not involve screens and servers, having in-person contact, with group activities, is going to be the best environment for development and flourishing.

On the Infed website there are a number of articles about how we might move forward, all around these three concepts: sanctuary, community and hope. These seem to me to be good themes to look at here.

Sanctuary

I wrote about this in 2017 and the words written then are even more relevant now:

> Historically, places of sanctuary were those where a person could find refuge, acceptance and care for any number of different reasons. They were cities of refuge, and then later, often Monasteries. Still today you can turn up a monastery (there were more of them then than now) and ask for shelter and sanctuary and they will give you what you need. They were used by those in trouble, those with difficult decisions to make, those for whom decisions were being taken that they didn't want to be a part of. They were places of community, protection and wisdom. Once you had entered the church/monastery building, you were under God's protection and no one could drag you out until the matter was settled.
>
> In today's context we need to see the concept of sanctuary being brought back where it has been lost; sanctuary as a temporary

place/time where a person takes time out, seeking the wisdom and protection of others, in order to find a solution or way forward from their present position. Young people need the church to be these places and times or even people. Young people who are struggling to find where they fit, to make decisions about their future, to get space to think about the multiple problems they are carrying, to find love and care for them in their anxiety or depression, need rest, refreshing, care, wisdom and protection; they need sanctuary.

I wrote about the church and this is still a good question about our church youth work: is it a place of sanctuary? If not, the question is: how can it become more like that? But this is also a challenge for all youth work practitioners, regardless of the context you work in. Mark Smith writes about the need to view sanctuary in two forms, sanctuary *for* and sanctuary *from*[9].

Sanctuary for includes the space to consider some big questions, to think deep thoughts and to be known. Sanctuary from includes fleeing spaces and places where identity is not recognised or where there might be troublesome relationships.

Each of these is a challenge in the current circumstances and because of this, will become all the more important in the future. All the youth workers I have spoken to in the course of writing this book recognise this need and would, to a lesser or greater degree, describe their youth work in these terms. Hot Chocolate and others with their commitment to asking young people questions and responding to their experiences and desires. Outward Bound with their In School Adventure programmes providing experiences in an outdoor context that are sanctuary from the grind of school life that it currently is. Juvenis and their work with young people in and around the justice system, providing a space for young people to connect with support. I could go on! Sanctuary has always been an important element of youth work; it is only going to become more so in the future.

Community

Humans beings do not survive well without community. There's a reason why solitary confinement is a punishment. A reason why we have all been feeling so disconnected and discombobulated during the covid era. A reason why social media has become such a prominent feature of our lives. Connection is important, the feeling of being connected with a community is essential to our sense of well-being. We've also all discovered just how much of community life we perhaps have taken for granted, the micro connections which all build a sense of shared connection. In the middle of the first lockdown, I had a conversation with my eldest boy about this, he was really struggling with the feeling of isolation and wailed at me 'I just want to see my friends, even if it's Billy!' Billy[10], for context, is a boy who used to call my boy names, who would stick his foot out in the corridor while my boy was passing, who routinely broke or stole new pens or pencils that my boy took into school.

That my boy was so desperate to see someone, he would be happy if that was the boy who was bullying him is baffling, until you consider how important micro-connections are. In his school there are 1200 pupils plus a whole team of teaching and support staff. In what now feels like a crazy system, the bell would ring and all 1200 pupils would leave their classroom and go to another one, sometimes on the same corridor but more often than not, a room on the other side of the school. And then, in another mad move, they would have two 30min breaks in which all 1200 pupils would pour out of classrooms into the dining hall or into the outside spaces!

Now, this school is blessed with a large playground, plus basketball courts and a large field, it is more than enough space for all 1200 of them. However, all this moving around means micro-connections with a significant chunk of the school community and this would happen 8 times a day. One of the biggest consequences of the first lockdown was the complete cessation of this. There was a lot that was unprecedented about that first lockdown, but for my eldest boy, an extrovert who needs people, this was the biggest challenge.

We cannot let online completely supplant the building of community, the micro-connections which create our community are imperative, as are the more intentional connections of friends and family around us. Community is a common theme in youth work projects and there are many who have connected with even more young people in their locality as a result of the pandemic. Urban Devotion found themselves involved in delivering food right across Birmingham. Listen Threads wellbeing packages now reach beyond the small group of those involved in the social enterprise work. Lucy at St James' in Clitheroe, built community by welcoming all those who want to be part of the youth band.

Hope

Right at the beginning of this book we talked about how essential hope is, the feeling of hopelessness is a mark of poor mental health, especially over an extended period of time and for good reason. As humans respond well to community, we also respond well when there is hope! In the news recently we heard about a surge in holiday bookings purportedly from the over 50s as the news about vaccines being rolled out in larger numbers gains traction. It's being dubbed 'vaccine confidence' and it's an important sign for industry leaders. The BBC quoted the boss of TUI saying "we are seeing glimmers of hope"[11]

For those with a faith, hope is a particularly well-articulated concept, both for the life we live now but also for a life after death. It is a powerful belief which is central to the Christian faith and mission and with good reason. Hope is an emotion, the opposite of fear. Hope is an intention or choice, to hope without action is to bring on hopelessness. Hope must be paired with action and in doing we both give ourselves a future and make the present more bearable. Hope is an intellectual activity, not just a feeling but a way of understanding ourselves and the world around us.[12] Christians use the language of hope frequently.

However, hope is an innate part of what it means to be human, we are a species who plans and looks forward and therefore it is an intrinsic part of our nature to have hope, whether we are people of faith or not. Awakening this hope in young people is a crucial role for us as youth workers, in the chapter on schools work we heard from Lynn McCann who talked about translating hope as an idea for autistic young people who find thinking in abstract impossible.

We must give hope to our young people, in these times when they are unhappy, not optimistic about the future, unable to make plans or see anything that might help them to consider what their futures might look like. We need to help them see what there is to hope for, remind them that the current situation will change, and to encourage them to use the voice they have and will have in the future to choose what our world looks like. It is hope in the capacity to change that drives people like Marcus Rashford, Greta Thunberg, David Attenborough, Jack Munroe, (who you might know as the Bootstrap Cook,) Extinction Rebellion and so many more, even politicians and civil servants.

The Great Outdoors

As we have discussed in this book, since the end of the first lockdown period in March 2020, the National Youth Agency has been central to the understanding of what can and cannot be done with young people during this pandemic. Even in the most restricted periods since May 2020, youth work outdoors has been permitted, in the form of detached work. In times of fewer restrictions, youth work has largely taken place outdoors, thanks mainly to the warm weather over the summer of 2020. Those delivering detached youth work training report an uptick in requests, there has been a rise generally in the offering of training for detached youth work alongside the online youth work provision. There is also a wealth of information about how getting young people outdoors can be so beneficial. I think it's worth some consideration here.

Maybe you think that outdoor youth work is for scouts and the like. You'll have read in the previous chapter about the work they are doing alongside the Woodcraft Folk and it's fairly likely one or two of your young people go to Scouts or Guides or similar as well as being part of your youth group. It may feel rather superfluous or even daunting to consider extending your youth work to an outdoor setting. Thoughts of Bear Grylls and The Island might be coming to mind right now! But I think that, like online youth work, working with young people outdoors is going to be a major permanent change in our practice. As we have spent nearly a year now in various stages of restrictions, a significant chunk of the time has come with a strong 'stay at home' message. Many young people, along with adults, have become anxious and lost their confidence about being outside. This needs to be rebuilt and those for whom this is their bread and butter, for The Outward Bound Trust, for Scouts, Woodcraft Folk, Sidewalk and others of this ilk you can be sure they will take every opportunity to resume face to face outdoors youth work.

For others who perhaps are not on familiar ground here and therefore are uncertain about lighting fires or leading treks; perhaps your context is very urban and lighting a fire in your local green space isn't going to go down well (please don't light fires in your local park!), worry not. It need not be this ambitious. In fact, one of the analogies I like the most about youth work is that it's more like gardening than carpentry[13]. It's more like nurturing green shoots of something you thought was a red tulip only to discover as it flowers that it's purple. More like seeing that your seedlings aren't doing so well in the full sunshine and moving them into some shade. Youth work is not building a solid structure, either as a master crafter or as a novice with instructions from Ikea.

Talk to the young people you love and care for, find out what they want to do outdoors and start there. All the better if you can get them noticing their surroundings, pausing to experience the awe and wonder of a beautiful building design or the colour of the sky at sunset. These are important experiences that will help to calm some of the anxiety, to lift their eyes up and begin to dream of a new world.

The Art of Reflective Practice

For those of you with a strong reflective practice streak you will, no doubt, already have done some of this work. Reflection helps us to see a way forward, helps us recognise that this is not a sprint but a marathon, and helps us realise how far we've come. If you've not tried it before then I would suggest that doing some reflection will help enormously. I'd recommend a tool like Now What, a tool for theological reflection by Youthscape[14] or The Year Compass[15].

When I asked the youth & community population on Twitter for some ideas on reflecting, here are the responses:

My first question is always, how are you?

How do we help each process the changes?

What have been some of the losses and disappointments this year?

What are you celebrating this year?

What is a hope you'll carry [forward]?

What have you learned?

What opportunities has it presented?

How has it felt?

What surprised you?

What felt really important a year ago? What feels really important now?

What did "success" look like a year ago? What does it look like now?

What have we learned about protecting and promoting our own wellbeing?

What have we learned about protecting and promoting the wellbeing of young people in what we do and how we do it?

Practicing the art of reflection is essential to the longevity of any youth worker, whichever sector they are working in; carving out the time for it will improve your own wellbeing, your working practices and your ability to stay at it for the long term.

And finally

We cannot truly know what the future holds, this covid era has shown us that, has exacerbated the unknown and brought it right up close! As has been said numerous times in the last year: we are all in the same storm, but not all in the same boat.

As we continue to navigate the ups and downs of living in the midst of a pandemic, including all the anxiety and overwhelm which comes with that we need to continue to look forward with hope, trust and a commitment to making sure our young people know what it is to be part of a community, to have hope and to know sanctuary.

Whether you are working in faith-based youth work or not, now is the time to dig deep; to keep on ensuring that the work we are doing is supporting those who most need it. This does not mean we should be running on empty; we must make sure we give ourselves the time and space we need to rest and recharge our own batteries.

We need to pay heed to those people who have been telling us to manage our time well, to keep good reflective records and to make use of a mentor, coach or therapist for regular opportunities to offload and process our own thoughts and feelings.

Let's commit to laying some foundations during this time which will help us rebuild a world where the hungry are fed, the poor are clothed and the marginalised are lifted up. A world that recognises the potential for change that our young people bring, a world that truly embraces, cares for and listens to those who will shape our future.

LIST OF ALL CONTRIBUTORS

Joe Lowther, KICK

Lynn McCann, ReachOutASC

Natalie Harling, The Outward Bound Trust

Dave Johnson, MINE Youth, New Castle

Steve Blower, Sidewalk, Scarborough

Charis Robertson, Hot Chocolate

Helen Perry, Worth Unlimited Waltham Forest

Jane Barrett & Chloe Latham, Listen Threads

Andy Winmill, Urban Devotion

Alison Mawby, KPC Youth

Winston Goode, Juvenis

Paul Burns, 1st Addington Scouts

Charlie Smith, West Yorkshire Fire and Rescue Service: Youth Interventions team

Jen Claire, Cub leader

Claire Stewart, Carnelea Methodist Church, Bangor, Northern Ireland

Alastair Middlemist, Maidstone Baptist Church, Maidstone

Lucy Skelton, St James' Clitheroe

Loyd Harp, Rudgwick Youth Centre, Horsham

Lizzy Iysaght, Red Balloon Foundation

Lee Wright, Grassroots Cardiff

NOTES

Introduction

1. A note about the language this book uses. There has been long debate about the use of the term 'youth work' or, for those in a particularly Christian faith context, 'youth ministry'. I have settled on using the term youth work as it encompasses more across a wide spectrum of activity which, for the most part, includes working with young people in a faith or church-based context.
2. https://www.wired.co.uk/article/future-of-zoom accessed 2nd Jan 2021
3. https://www.theguardian.com/world/2020/oct/12/englands-three-tier-covid-system-brings-much-needed-clarity accessed 29th Dec 2020
4. https://youngminds.org.uk/about-us/reports/coronavirus-impact-on-young-people-with-mental-health-needs/ accessed 29th Dec 2020
5. There are different organisations which perform this umbrella role in the different countries of the UK: the NYA covers England, YouthLink Scotland, YouthLink Northern Ireland, and the Council for Wales of Voluntary Youth Services cover their respective countries.

1. Strengthen Community - Working in Schools

1. I'm aware that not everyone agrees on the appropriate way to address those who are autistic. However, Lynn MacCann, of ReachOutASC, expressly asked me to use 'autistic people' rather than 'people with autism' so that is what I'll do.
2. Do take a look at their website www.kick.org.uk and get in touch with Joe and the team if you want to find out more.
3. The Outward Bound Trust Report "HELPING YOUNG PEOPLE RECONNECT, REBUILD AND RECHARGE DURING THE COVID-19 PANDEMIC" 2020 available from their website.
4. Take a look at this short paper for more details https://network.autism.org.uk/knowledge/insight-opinion/double-empathy-problem accessed 22 Dec 2020

2. Wilderness Prophets - Detached Youth Work
Stories

1. The Albemarle Report: activities and facilities, infed.org https://infed.org/mobi/the-albemarle-report-activities-and-facilities/ accessed 31st Dec 2020
2. Available here https://www.fdyw.org.uk/post/detached-youth-work-guidance-june-2020 accessed 31st Dec 2020

3. MINE Youth Christmas News December 2020

3. Faith As Its Purpose - Church Based Youth Work Stories

1. Find out more about this here https://www.youthscape.co.uk/nymw accessed 11th Jan 2021
2. Find out more about this here https://www.youthscape.co.uk/satellites accessed 11th Jan 2021
3. Shepherd, Nick (2016) Faith Generation SPCK London quote from page 6

4. Embedded - Youth & Community Work Stories

1. This article explains this phenomenon, though I'm less than pleased as a Gen Xer myself to be lumped together with the Boomer Generation as Lindsey does here! https://lindseypollak.com/breaking-down-generational-perspectives-on-phone-calls-face-to-face-conversations-and-promotions/ accessed 1st Dec 2020
2. Juvenis Impact Report 2018 – 19 from www.juvenis.org.uk accessed 1st Dec 2020

5. Embodied Faith - Christian Youth Work Charity Stories

1. TLG Make Lunch are a charity who enable and equip churches to provide free meals to children and families who would otherwise go hungry. You can find out more about this on their website https://www.tlg.org.uk/your-church/make-lunch

6. New Adventures - Outdoor Youth Work

1. https://www.theguardian.com/society/2019/jun/16/girls-join-scouts-in-record-numbers-beavers-cubs accessed 12th Jan 2021
2. ibid
3. https://youtu.be/Cz7JoRQmaBs The 'BIGG' Challenge 2020 Promo Video – Biggleswade District Scouts
4. https://www.theguardian.com/society/2020/jun/05/scout-troops-pair-up-with-care-homes-across-uk#:~:text=Scout%20troops%20are%20being%20paired,solidarity%20with%20the%20most%20vulnerable. Accessed 12th Jan 2021
5. https://woodcraft.org.uk/about accessed 12th Jan 2021
6. https://dreambigathome.uk/ accessed 12th Jan 2021

7. Quoted in The Outward Bound Trust Report: Helping Young People Reconnect, Rebuild and Recharge During the Covid-19 Pandemic August – December 2020 available from the website www.outwardbound.org.uk accessed 20th Jan 2021
8. As before

7. To Zoom or Not to Zoom? - Online youth work

1. https://www.distractify.com/p/what-happened-to-aol-mail   accessed   18th Jan 2021
2. This article does a good job of summarising this,https://www.thetimes.co.uk/ article/hold-me-tighter-the-new-science-of-touch-xclm6rsj6   accessed   18th Jan 2021
3. https://www.wired.co.uk/article/future-of-zoom accessed 2nd Jan 2021
4. https://www.entrepreneur.com/article/359786 accessed 18th Jan 2021
5. https://mediakix.com/blog/celebrity-influencer-marketing-instagram-examples/ accessed 18th Jan 2021
6. https://www.statista.com/statistics/264810/number-of-monthly-active-facebook-users-worldwide/#:~:text=With%20over%202.7%20billion%20monthly,network%20ever%20to%20do%20so. Accessed 18th Jan 2021
7. From Youth Work in a Time of Covid – July and August diaries: We Are Seeing the Value of Youth Work – Youth & Policy https://www.youthandpolicy.org/ articles/youth-work-in-a-time-of-covid2 accessed 18th Jan 2021
8. Available from www.grovebooks.co.uk search for Tim Gough in the Youth section

8. Where do we go from here?

1. https://www.unicef.org.uk/publications/report-card-11-child-wellbeing-what-do-you-think/ accessed 13th Jan 2021
2. Smith, M.K. (2020) Dealing with the 'new normal'. Offering Sanctuary, community and hope to children and young people in schools and local organizations. *The encyclopedia of pedagogy and informal education.* [https://infed.org/mobi/dealing-with-the-new-normal-creating-places-of-sanctuary=community-and-hope-for-children-and-young-people/ accessed 13th Jan 2021]
3. It is worth pointing out that a true ABCD approach is most effective when used in very specific local community contexts. However, I think the overall approach of looking for the good things rather than beginning with the need or negatives will be useful here.
4. Rashford talks candidly about this in this article in The Guardian https://www. theguardian.com/football/2020/nov/02/burberry-partners-with-marcus-rashford-to-fund-youth-centres accessed 14th Jan 2021
5. Marcus Rashford MBE on Twitter 13 Jan 2021 – Marcus received the Member of the British Empire award in the New Years Honours List of 2021
6. https://time.com/5463721/most-influential-teens-2018 accessed 14th Jan 2021

7. Smith, M.K. (2020) Dealing with the 'new normal'. Offering Sanctuary, community and hope to children and young people in schools and local organizations. *The encyclopedia of pedagogy and informal education.* [https://infed.org/mobi/dealing-with-the-new-normal-creating-places-of-sanctuary=community-and-hope-for-children-and-young-people/ accessed 13th Jan 2021]

8. Klein, Naomi (2020) Screen New Deal. Under Cover of Mass Death, Andrew Cuomo Calls in the Billionaires to Build a High-Tech Dystopia, *The Intercept* 8th May [https://theintercept.com/2020/05/08/andrew-cuomo-eric-schmidt-coronavirus-tech-shock-doctrine/ accessed 13th Jan 2021]

9. Smith, M.K. (2020) Dealing with the 'new normal'. Offering Sanctuary, community and hope to children and young people in schools and local organizations. *The encyclopedia of pedagogy and informal education.* [https://infed.org/mobi/dealing-with-the-new-normal-creating-places-of-sanctuary=community-and-hope-for-children-and-young-people/ accessed 13th Jan 2021]

10. This name has been changed

11. https://www.bbc.co.uk/news/business-55654127 accessed 14th Jan 2021

12. Smith, M.K. (2020) Dealing with the 'new normal'. Offering Sanctuary, community and hope to children and young people in schools and local organizations. *The encyclopedia of pedagogy and informal education.* [https://infed.org/mobi/dealing-with-the-new-normal-creating-places-of-sanctuary=community-and-hope-for-children-and-young-people/ accessed 13th Jan 2021]

13. Full disclosure: this is not my analogy, neither am I a gardener! I believe the analogy came from the Infed website www.infed.org.uk

14. Available here https://www.youthscape.co.uk/store/product/now-what

15. Available here https://yearcompass.com/

ACKNOWLEDGMENTS

I would like to thank:

Everyone I spoke to, everyone who sent me information and contacts or suggestions of who to talk to, that saying 'it takes a village to raise a child' definitely applies in this case.

My family for getting on with life while I plug away at this writing game.

Dave Roberts for encouraging me to begin and talking me through all the nitty gritty to get this published.

My Get It Done group of wonderful human beings who have also read, reflected, encouraged and generally been fantastic people.